ALL ABOUT ADAM

Teacher Paris Ford hopes to improve the performances of Brockton College's basketball team. But going to the new athletic director for help, she's confronted by the startlingly handsome Adam Kincaid. Years ago, Paris secretly witnessed Adam's role in her family's scandal and she isn't about to forgive or forget. However, Adam's tender kisses melt her resolve to maintain a professional relationship. Now she must discover the truth about Adam's past and look toward a future ... with the man she loved.

MS

MOYRA TARLING

ALL ABOUT ADAM

Complete and Unabridged

LINFORD
Leicester

First published in the United States of America
in 1991

First Linford Edition
published 2012

British Library CIP Data

Tarling, Moyra.
   All about Adam.- -(Linford romance library)
   1. Love stories.
   2. Large type books.
   I. Title II. Series
   823.9′2–dc23

   ISBN 978–1–4448–0967–1

Published by
F. A. Thorpe (Publishing)
Anstey, Leicestershire

Set by Words & Graphics Ltd.
Anstey, Leicestershire
Printed and bound in Great Britain by
T. J. International Ltd., Padstow, Cornwall

This book is printed on acid-free paper

To Mary,
who liked this story from the start!

1

Paris Ford pulled her old red Volkswagen into the parking lot allocated for college staff members and brought it to a halt.

Grabbing her briefcase from the passenger seat, she climbed out and stood shivering in the chill of the January morning.

She pulled the collar of her coat up around her ears and smiled fleetingly, remembering the sunshine and warmth she'd left behind in Hawaii only the day before. But the holidays were over, and now she was wishing she'd returned home a few days earlier and given herself more time to acclimatize to the freezing January temperatures of the Oregon coast.

Her appointment with George Boone, athletic director at Brockton College, had been scheduled for eight o'clock. She glanced at the watch on her wrist and saw that it was now five minutes past the hour.

'Damn!' Paris closed the car door and hurried toward the administration building. The campus, like a sleepy bear after hibernation, was growling noisily as students made their way to early classes.

Paris tried to focus her thoughts on the interview ahead. She'd had an appointment to see George Boone the morning before the college closed for the Christmas holidays, but he'd been called away and she'd had to reschedule it, for this morning.

In the two week interim, she'd had ample time to rethink her position. As a new member of the staff, she was more than a little reluctant to voice her concerns, but she'd felt strongly that it was necessary. She owed it to her students.

She pushed open the large glass doors of the administration building and was immediately glad of the warmth curling around her. She took the elevator to the fifth floor. Stepping out into the carpeted reception area, she was struck by the unusual silence. Normally at this time in the morning, the two typists were hard at work and Marjorie Stusiak, George Boone's secretary, was seated at her desk looking sharp and efficient.

Today, there was no one in sight.

Frowning, Paris approached Marjorie's desk and noticed the flashing lights on the telephone indicating several incoming calls. Placing her briefcase at her feet, Paris removed her woolen coat and dropped it on one of the chairs nearby.

She tucked a strand of short blond hair behind her ear and gazed at the solid oak door at the end of the hallway to her right. Behind the door was George Boone's office.

Indecision kept her rooted to the spot for several more seconds, but then she reminded herself that she had to be in class in another twenty minutes. Bending down, she picked up her briefcase and made her way down the hallway.

The door was slightly ajar, and just as she was about to knock, the door opened and she stumbled forward and found herself up against the solid wall of a man's chest.

'What the hell!' A rich, vibrant voice muttered in her ear and a pair of strong hands steadied her.

Paris gasped at the contact and her fingers loosened their hold on her briefcase, which landed with a dull thud on the carpeted floor.

'I'm sorry.' The apology came automatically to her lips. Lifting her head, she found herself staring into a pair of honey-gold eyes, framed by dark, chocolate-brown lashes. Recognition flashed through her and hastily she took a step back.

'What the devil do you think you're doing, barging in here without knocking?' he asked angrily.

Paris blinked twice trying to clear her vision. Her heart began to kick alarmingly against her ribs as Adam Kincaid's features came into sharp focus. Devastating, powerful, and outrageously attractive — he was all of that, and more. Though she hadn't seen him in twelve years, Paris felt a strong pull of attraction that drew a response from deep inside her.

Staring at the broad expanse of chest hidden under an immaculate pinstriped suit and crisp, cotton shirt, Paris suddenly understood, for the first time in her life, how her cousin Francesca could have fallen in love with this man. But his callous treatment had destroyed her cousin's life, and Adam Kincaid had walked away from the mess scot-free.

'I have an appointment with Mr. Boone,' she said, managing, with difficulty, to suppress the feeling of anger and resentment threatening to surface.

She deliberately ignored the way her pulse was racing, telling herself her reaction was simply a result of the shock of the collision and nothing more.

'An appointment,' Adam repeated,

letting his eyes roam over the woman before him. Almost as tall as he, she looked stunningly attractive in an apple green cowl-necked sweater and black wool skirt. Her eyes were the exact shade of the sweater and her face had a tanned, healthy glow that had him suddenly thinking of sun-kissed beaches and hot summer days. 'Would you mind telling me who you are?' he asked, and watched in fascination as her tongue appeared to moisten lips that were full and sensual.

'My name is Paris Ford. I teach English and commercial arts,' she told him, finding her voice and her control. 'Where's Mr. Boone?' she asked, glancing around the room. But there was no sign of the man she'd come to see.

'I'm Adam Kincaid. George Boone is my uncle,' he told her, then swallowed before continuing. 'He's in the intensive care unit at the hospital. He suffered a heart attack yesterday afternoon.'

'A heart attack!' Paris was stunned.

'I'm so sorry,' she said, her tone sincere. 'I had no idea. I've been in Hawaii. I got back last night. Is he going to be all right?'

'It was touch and go for a while, but he's doing as well as can be expected.' Adam repeated the words he'd been told a few minutes ago when he'd telephoned the hospital. 'What did you want to see him about?' He was reluctant to let his thoughts linger on his uncle, the man who'd been like a father to him. But George was a fighter, Adam reminded himself. He'd make it. He had to.

'I wanted to ask his advice,' Paris explained, noting the look of worry and tension on Adam Kincaid's features. Fleetingly, she found herself wondering how George Boone's wife Lillian was doing, but before she could ask, Adam spoke again.

'I'm the new assistant athletic director. I'll be taking over for my uncle,' he said, his tone brusque and businesslike as he moved to stand behind the large oak desk. 'Perhaps I can help?'

Paris hesitated, letting her glance drift past Adam to the window and to the snowflakes beginning to fall outside. She was suddenly reluctant to voice her concerns, and yet she felt she'd put the matter on hold long enough.

Adam Kincaid's voice cut through her thoughts. 'If you're thinking of waiting until my uncle returns, don't.' There was impatience in his tone now. 'He'll be out of the picture for some time. If there's something on your mind, I suggest you tell me what it is.'

Paris brought her gaze back to Adam and noted with apprehension the look of frustration and anger in his gold-speckled eyes.

She cleared her throat. 'Very well,' she said. 'I made this appointment in order to draw Mr. Boone's attention to half a dozen students who take my English classes. None of those students are doing the work I assign. Some are skipping my classes altogether, and all six of them seem to take it for granted that I'll simply hand them out a passing grade

8

regardless of what they do.' Paris stopped and watched Adam Kincaid's face for a reaction. There was none.

'This sounds like a disciplinary problem to me, Miss Ford, and not something that need be brought to this department's attention.'

Paris bristled at the condescending tone of his voice. Strangely she felt disappointed at his reaction, but that emotion was quickly pushed aside and replaced by another.

'A disciplinary problem . . . ' She repeated the phrase he'd used, trying to hold on to her temper. 'I see,' she said, shaking her head in disbelief. 'Do you really believe that if this . . . if this was simply a disciplinary problem, I would be here?'

She was angry. He could see it in the bright glitter of her eyes, and in the pink glow of her cheeks.

'You've given me no indication that it's anything more than that,' he stated calmly. She was new to the college — that much was evident, for he was sure he would have remembered if he'd seen her at the graduation ceremonies in June. And she had a young, rather innocent look about her, which to him was a telltale sign that she was also new to teaching.

'How long have you been teaching college, Miss Ford?' Adam Kincaid suddenly asked.

'This is my first year,' she replied.

'Then this must be your first job.'

'That's right,' she said. 'But what has that to do with anything?' Resentment crept into her voice. With an M.A. in English Literature, she was well qualified for the post.

'Listen, Miss Ford. Until my uncle is back on his feet and behind this desk, I'll be running this department, and at the moment I don't have time to deal with petty grievances.'

The telephone on his desk began to ring. 'Excuse me,' he said, picking up the receiver. 'Kincaid, here,' he said, then he listened for several moments. 'Yes. Hold on a moment.' Placing his hand over the mouthpiece, he looked toward her. 'Is there anything else?'

Paris swallowed the biting retort that came to mind. 'Not a thing,' she said. Turning, she retrieved her briefcase, and without a backward glance, she strode from the room.

Inside she was fuming. He hadn't given her a chance to explain that the six students causing the problems were all members of the basketball team. Nor had he been interested in knowing that several of the senior students had begun a subtle campaign of intimidation.

Ignoring Marjorie Stusiak's greeting, she stormed down the hallway, thankful that the elevator doors slid open.

Without as much as a by-your-leave, Adam Kincaid had implied that the problems in her classroom had to do with her own teaching skills and nothing more. Granted, she was a new teacher, but none of the students in any of her other classes were a problem — only the ones who were members of the basketball team.

She couldn't help feeling that if George Boone had been there, he would have listened more sympathetically, perhaps made some inquiries of his own. But not Adam Kincaid. He had dismissed her and her problem swiftly and effectively, just as he'd dismissed her cousin, Francesca, twelve years ago.

The anger she'd forced herself to suppress moments ago washed over her, and it was all she could do to stop herself from returning to the director's office to tell Adam Kincaid exactly what she thought of him.

By the time she reached her classroom, reason had returned, and as she quieted the noisy mob of thirty-odd young men and women, she pushed all thoughts of Adam Kincaid from her mind.

* * *

The rest of the week proved to be overly long and decidedly tedious, and Paris was thankful when Friday afternoon arrived at last. As she made her way to the staff room in the north building, she reflected that the main topic of conversation all week had centered around George Boone and his heart attack, as well as the new acting athletic director, Adam Kincaid. Paris heard only accolades and praise for Adam Kincaid, and it had grown increasingly difficult for her to smile and nod at these comments.

As she rounded the last corner and headed for the staff room, she found herself walking toward Adam Kincaid, who was coming from the opposite direction. She bristled, every muscle tensing at the sight of him.

'Miss Ford,' he acknowledged, as they reached the door together.

'Mr. Kincaid,' Paris said, keeping her expression guarded. Her heart, on the other hand, seemed intent on behaving erratically, jumping crazily against her rib cage.

He held the door for her, and as she moved past him her gaze lifted to meet his. In that fleeting moment, Paris felt as if the air had suddenly been snatched from her lungs. Her mouth went dry and a strange prickly sensation danced across her skin.

She saw something flicker in the depths of his eyes before it disappeared. 'Thank you,' she muttered, as she hurried toward the table where the coffee maker and mugs sat.

Dropping her briefcase and an armful of papers onto a nearby chair, she reached for a coffee mug. With hands that were trembling, she began to fill it.

There was only a smattering of teachers in the staff room — the Friday afternoon influx had not yet begun — and behind her she could hear Adam acknowledge their greetings.

Only after she'd taken several sips of the dark brown liquid was she able to turn and glance in his direction. He was standing by the window talking to Raymond Chancellor, one of the college's history professors. Raymond was in his mid-fifties with bright blue eyes and a shock of white hair. He was a man well loved and respected by staff and students alike.

And that included Paris. She couldn't forget how he'd taken her under his wing those first weeks at the beginning of term, and helped her to settle into the college way of life. She discovered that being a teacher was different from being a student, and it had taken a little time to make the adjustment.

Lillian Boone, the athletic director's wife, had also been exceedingly kind and unfailingly helpful during those first weeks. Paris had liked the older woman's friendly attitude and the way she treated the staff like one large family. During the past week Paris tried to telephone Lillian without success, and she wished now she'd thought a moment ago to ask Adam Kincaid how the director's wife was coping.

As the room slowly began to fill, Paris realized that the majority of staff liked and respected Adam Kincaid. A few minutes later, when he raised his voice above the chatter and asked for their attention, everyone quickly complied.

'I'd just like to take this opportunity to let you all know that George is in stable condition and is slowly beginning to show signs of improvement. When I drop by the hospital later, I'll pass on all your good wishes.' He scanned the room, his glance coming to rest on Paris.

'Oh, and I'd like to thank you all for the support and cooperation you've given me throughout this rather hectic week.' He held her gaze for a long moment and his mouth curled into a small smile.

Paris quickly turned away to hide the feeling of annoyance flickering through her. That he was mocking her was obvious, and just for a moment she was tempted to confront him with her problem once again in front of everyone. But he'd already given her his answer, and after his rather abrupt treatment of her in George Boone's office on Tuesday morning, she'd made a point of avoiding him.

She would just have to find a way to resolve the situation herself. Perhaps she should try talking to Stuart Unger, the head basketball coach, once more. This thought brought a shudder of distaste chasing across her skin. When she'd approached Unger prior to Christmas break to talk to him about the players' grades, he'd laughed at her. That's when she'd made the appointment with George Boone.

'There is one more thing,' Adam went on. 'I've been asked to mention that the wine-and-cheese party scheduled for tonight has been canceled. It will be re-scheduled at a later date. Thank you.'

Paris bent to retrieve her briefcase and papers. Her intention was to leave, but noticing that Adam Kincaid was making his way toward the staff room door, she hesitated.

'Hey, Paris! Don't run away yet!'

Paris turned to see Lucy Reynolds,

17

one of the secretaries in the administration office, bearing down on her. 'I haven't had a chance to talk to you all week. How was Christmas in Hawaii?' Lucy asked, dropping into the armchair next to Paris.

'Hot!' Paris replied with a smile.

'Lucky duck,' said her friend. 'It snowed here on Christmas Eve, just like it is now. I sat in front of the fire thinking of you, suntanning on the beach.'

'I didn't have much time for suntanning,' Paris told her. 'My mother insisted on dragging me to every dress shop in Honolulu to try on a hundred different bridesmaid dresses. If your mother ever says she's getting married again, tell her to elope,' Paris advised.

'How did the wedding go?' Lucy asked.

'Without a hitch. It was simply wonderful,' Paris breathed, her thoughts drifting back over the emotional wedding ceremony that had been held outdoors in the immense and exotic gardens of the estate belonging to her new stepfather.

'What's your mother's new husband like?'

'Very nice. Devilishly handsome, for a man of sixty-five,' Paris said, repeating the description her mother had used the first time she'd told Paris about Robert Craig.

'Speaking of handsome,' Lucy said, lowering her voice a little. 'What do you think of Adam Kincaid? Isn't he a hunk?'

Paris let her gaze shift to where Raymond Chancellor stood talking with two other professors. She smiled and waved a greeting, giving herself time to think of a suitable reply to Lucy's question. 'He's all right, I suppose,' she said carefully, unwilling to let her friend know that she found the man annoyingly arrogant and uncaringly rude.

'*All right?*' Lucy's tone was indignant. 'Paris, you must be blind. He's gorgeous — but then, I've always thought so. Not that it's done me any good. He comes back every June to attend the graduation ceremonies, but in the five years I've been working here he's never given me anything more than a passing glance.' She stopped and studied Paris for a moment. 'With your blond hair and slim figure . . . I'd say you're more his type,' she added, flashing Paris a teasing smile.

'Not in a million years,' Paris said with such stark certainty that Lucy looked at her in surprise.

'Methinks the lady doth protest too much . . . ' Lucy said, a twinkle of amusement in her brown eyes.

Paris said nothing, annoyed that she'd allowed her anger at Adam Kincaid to show through. 'You've got the quote wrong, Lucy . . . ' she began, her intention to shift the conversation in another direction.

Lucy readily obliged. 'Never mind quoting chapter and verse to me,' she said with a laugh. 'Just because you're a literary genius . . . Listen, I'd better go,' she continued hurriedly, glancing toward the window. 'Just look at that snow coming down. You should have stayed in Hawaii,' she added, raising her hand in a wave.

'See you Monday,' Paris said as she began to gather her briefcase and papers and make her way toward the closet where, during lunch break, she'd hung her coat.

Five minutes later, as she carefully negotiated her way across the parking lot, she frowned at the huge white flakes drifting down from the somber sky.

What would the roads be like? she wondered. It had been snowing all day and there was an accumulation of at least four inches on the ground. The small house she was renting was located on a rather isolated stretch of road a mile out of town, and she was beginning to wonder if her car would make it home.

She hadn't thought about winter road conditions when she'd come to Brockton in the summer to look for a place to stay. After a week of tramping around town with the housing agent looking at furnished and unfurnished apartments near the campus, she hadn't

21

found anything she liked.

It wasn't until she'd commented that she much preferred the kind of privacy a house afforded, that the agent had told her about the tiny house on the outskirts of town.

She'd fallen in love with it instantly, and the fact that the monthly rental had been a figure well within her budget had been an added bonus. But now, looking at the snow on the ground, Paris began to wonder if she shouldn't have opted for a place at least within walking distance to the college.

Already beginning to feel apprehensive about the drive home she set her briefcase in the snow and fumbled in her purse for her keys. She'd intended to purchase a set of snow tires for her car, but with the hectic rush before Christmas she hadn't gotten around to it, and up until today the weather hadn't been too bad.

She opened the car door and with a sigh tossed her briefcase, papers and purse into the passenger seat. Just as she was about to climb in, a voice broke the stillness, startling her.

'Miss Ford . . . ' The words were an urgent whisper.

Paris felt her heart slam against her ribs. She turned to see who was there. 'Neil! You scared me,' she exclaimed, as she recognized the young man before her. She relaxed and smiled at Neil Pavan, one of her students. He was a freshman and one of the college's new rising young basketball players.

'I'm sorry, Miss Ford, I didn't mean to frighten you,' Neil said, drawing nearer.

'That's all right. Is there something you wanted?' she asked.

'I . . . ' he began, then glanced around nervously. 'I just wanted you to know that I'm sorry about the hassle the other players have been giving you.'

Tension tightened within her as Paris studied Neil. At six foot three, he was in some respects short for a basketball player. But what he lacked in height, he made up for in skill, effort and energy. 'Your apology is welcome, Neil,' she said. 'But if you think that's all it takes to get your grade changed, then — '

'No, I don't expect anything,' he quickly cut in. His glance flickered from left to right, and in the eerie whiteness created by the falling snow, Paris saw a look of fear in the young man's eyes.

'Is something wrong?' she asked, a note of concern in her voice as she leaned toward him.

Neil thrust his hands into the pockets of his ski jacket and gazed at her for a long moment. He opened his mouth to speak, but suddenly the crunch of footsteps on the snow fractured the silence. Neil's head snapped to the right and Paris noted the look of apprehension that crossed his features.

She followed Neil's gaze, glancing at the approaching figure. Though he wore a dark coat, Paris had no trouble recognizing the man striding purposefully toward them. It was Adam Kincaid. Her eyes darted back to Neil and she was surprised to see he was already beginning to back away.

'It's nothing,' Neil mumbled. 'Forget it,' he added as he blended into the darkness.

'Neil! Wait!' Paris called after him, but Neil was no longer in sight.

2

'Is anything wrong?' Adam asked, his voice cutting through the chilly night air.

Paris turned to the man who'd just joined her. 'No, nothing's wrong,' she told him, ignoring the way her pulse kicked into high gear as her glance registered on his thick brown hair glistening with wet snowflakes. He'd turned up the collar of his heavy coat to protect him from the winter's icy wind, and somehow he looked mysterious and incredibly attractive.

'A friend of yours?' he asked, nodding in the direction Neil had taken.

'A student,' she told him wondering once more at Neil's unusual behavior.

'I wondered if perhaps you were having trouble with your car,' Adam said, turning to her once more. In truth, he'd thought she was in more

26

serious trouble. He'd recognized her the moment he'd left the administration building. There was no mistaking her tall, elegant figure or short blond hair. But when he caught sight of the second figure standing by the car, he'd had the impression they were arguing. He'd deliberately lengthened his stride in order to reach her.

'No, my car's fine,' she assured him. 'I just had the engine tuned about a month ago.' She moved to the open door of her car and slipped into the driver's seat.

She put the key in the ignition and turned it, but the engine didn't kick into life as she'd expected. In fact, there was no sound at all.

She glanced at Adam Kincaid standing nearby and frowned in puzzlement, even as she turned the key once more. Nothing . . . absolutely nothing. She couldn't believe it. Closing her eyes, Paris said a silent prayer and tried again.

'If I were you, I'd find a new garage,'

Adam said. 'I can give you a ride home,' he offered.

'That's all right. I'll call the road service,' Paris said, wishing with all her heart it was a warm day in June, rather than a snowy evening in January.

'On a night like this, I imagine they're pretty busy,' Adam said. 'Anyway, it's too cold to argue. Grab whatever you need. My car's right over there.' He pointed to the dark sedan parked directly opposite.

'You wouldn't happen to have a set of jumper cables, would you?' Paris asked, in one last-ditch effort, still puzzled by the fact that her car wouldn't start.

'Sorry.' His mouth curled into a small smile, and he was amused that she seemed determined to avoid his company. 'You could always walk, of course,' he added, and when he glimpsed the beginnings of a smile on her face, he felt something stir deep inside him.

'I'll just take my purse,' she said, having the good grace to accept. 'I'll get the rest of my things tomorrow.'

Paris crossed to Adam Kincaid's car and bit back a sigh as she sank down in the passenger seat. At the first turn of the key, his car's engine purred to life, and soon the heater was blowing warm air at her cold limbs.

Carefully maneuvering the car from the snow-covered parking lot, Adam pulled into the road that led away from the college.

'Where to?' he asked, his eyes on the road ahead.

'I live at the north end of Devon Park Road. Do you know where that is?'

'I know where it is,' he replied, casting a brief glance at her. 'But if I recall correctly, there isn't much out there.'

'There's one tiny old house,' Paris told him, wondering for the second time that evening why she'd chosen that particular place to reside.

'Oh, yes,' Adam said, his tone full of warm recollection. 'The old Bailey place. It's been empty for a long time. That's quite a way out. Whatever made you decide to live there?'

'I like it,' she said, a defensive note in her voice. 'The house has a lot more character than the apartments I looked at, and besides, the rent doesn't put a dent in my budget.'

At her words Adam slanted a lopsided grin in her direction and for the first time in her life, Paris knew the meaning of the phrase, *her heart skipped a beat.*

'Would you mind very much if I made a stop first?' he asked.

'Not at all,' Paris replied.

'I promised Aunt Lillian I'd drop by the hospital tonight to see how George is doing,' Adam explained.

'How is your aunt?' Paris asked, concerned for the woman who'd been so kind to her.

Adam flashed a glance at Paris. 'Not good, I'm afraid,' he said. 'George is her whole world. This has shaken her up rather badly.'

'I'm so sorry,' Paris said. She'd heard the note of despair in Adam's voice, and as she glanced at his profile in the dim light, she could see small lines of worry at the corner of his mouth.

Her own father had died of a heart attack five years before, and she could still recall how utterly helpless she'd felt as she'd watched his life ebb away. Tears filled her eyes at the memory and she blinked them away. 'George Boone seems like a fighter to me,' she said softly. 'If he's off the critical list, there's a good chance he'll make a good recovery.'

Surprised at the emotion he could hear in her voice, Adam glanced fleetingly at the woman beside him, noticing that her lovely green eyes were moist with unshed tears. As he turned his attention back to the road ahead, he found he had to fight the urge to reach out and touch her.

'Your uncle and aunt ... they've both been so kind and helpful since I joined the staff,' Paris went on sincerely. 'If there's anything I can do, please let me know.'

'Do you mean that?' he asked.

'Of course,' she replied, annoyed that he should ask such a question.

'Then there is something you can do,' Adam said, drawing her gaze to his face.

'Name it!'

'Well . . . Lillian is close to exhaustion herself. She's been at George's bedside from early morning to quite late at night throughout the past week. The nurses have a devil of a time getting her to go home. Perhaps you could come and talk some sense into her.'

'But why would she listen to me?' Paris asked.

'I don't know that she will,' he replied. 'But it's worth a try. When she sees me, she starts to cry. You see, I was with George in his study when he had the heart attack, and she can't seem to forget that. As far as she's concerned, her whole world has fallen apart. I understand how she feels but I'm worried that she's endangering her own health.'

Paris heard the love for his aunt, the depth of caring, in Adam's voice, and suddenly she felt drawn to this man, drawn to him in a way that surprised and frightened her.

'If you think it will help . . . I'll do what I can,' Paris added.

'Thank you.'

Paris turned her gaze to the snow falling outside, trying to convince herself that agreeing to help Adam Kincaid didn't constitute fraternizing with the enemy.

She watched the car's wipers as they swept the snowflakes aside, and her mind drifted back to the spring twelve years ago when she'd come to Brockton to stay with her Aunt Margaret and cousin Francesca.

Her father, a construction engineer, had taken a job for three months in the jungles of South America. Her mother had gone with him. Unwilling to take a twelve-year-old girl to that part of the world, they'd decided to leave Paris with her mother's sister, Margaret.

Paris hadn't minded being left behind. In fact, she'd been excited about spending several months with her cousin Francesca.

Though there was a six-year difference in their ages, they'd always gotten along well. An only child, Paris thought of Francesca as the sister she'd always wanted, and her cousin didn't seem to mind having an adoring fan — especially one who enjoyed being at her beck and call.

Francesca had been eighteen then, a sophomore at Brockton College, and a beautiful girl with shoulder-length black hair. Paris had envied Francesca's long hair and tall, slender figure, and wished she looked more like her cousin.

Each afternoon, Paris would race home from school, and when Francesca came in they'd spend several hours laughing and talking in her cousin's bedroom.

Paris was fascinated by the stories Francesca told of the young men at the college who were all eager to date her.

And from the way Francesca smiled and pranced around the room, Paris sensed that her cousin was very pleased by all the attention she was receiving.

But whenever Paris asked her if there was someone special that she liked, Francesca's expression would suddenly turn serious. There was someone she was madly and quite desperately in love with, she would say, but no matter how many times Paris asked his name, Francesca would always give a secret little smile and change the subject.

It was early May when Paris began to suspect that all was not well with her cousin. Their afternoon girl talk sessions had stopped, mainly because Francesca never arrived home much before supper time, and then she'd lock herself in her room without saying a word to anyone.

Aunt Margaret explained that Francesca was in the midst of exams and that she was studying, but Paris had sensed that there was another reason for her cousin's changed behavior.

Then late one evening, Paris woke to the sound of loud voices coming from the living room. Curious, she'd climbed out of bed and slowly crept down the stairs, coming to a halt when she heard the sound of her aunt's voice.

'But, Francesca! What are you going to do? How could you have allowed this to happen?' Aunt Margaret's voice was high-pitched and bordering on hysteria.

'Calm down, Mother. Everything will be all right, believe me,' Francesca replied, in an even tone.

'But how can you say that?' Paris heard her aunt ask.

'When I tell you who the father of my baby is, you'll understand,' came the reply.

Paris sat rigid with shock at Francesca's words. A baby? Francesca was going to have a baby!

'Who is the father?' Aunt Margaret asked, her voice echoing her despair.

There was a brief hesitation before her cousin spoke the name. 'Adam Kincaid.'

'Oh, my heavens!' Aunt Margaret's reply was a harsh whisper, and Paris frowned. It wasn't a name she recognized at all.

'Adam will marry me and everything will work out, you'll see,' Paris heard Francesca say in a somewhat self-satisfied tone.

'But he's a teacher at the college, isn't he?'

'He's a coach, Mother,' Francesca corrected. 'And because the college won't want a fuss, we'll probably just go off and get married quietly. Don't worry. I have everything under control.' There was a hint of smugness in her tone.

Paris heard the door to the living room open and instinctively, she jumped to her feet and hurried back to her room. Lying in bed, she'd tried to sort out in her own mind what Francesca had been talking about. If her cousin was going to have a baby and Adam Kincaid was the father, then Adam Kincaid must also be the man Francesca was desperately in love with, she'd concluded.

Paris slept late the next morning, and when she came downstairs to breakfast, Francesca had already left. Aunt Margaret seemed fretful and preoccupied, and unwilling to broach the subject with her aunt, Paris left for school, all her questions unanswered.

When she'd arrived home later that afternoon it was to find Francesca weeping hysterically and mumbling to Aunt Margaret that Adam had refused to marry her.

Throughout the disastrous weekend that followed, there were numerous telephone calls to the house. When Paris overheard Francesca say that Adam Kincaid was on his way over, she was anxious to see this cruel, uncaring man.

Though she'd been banished to her bedroom, Paris had crouched behind the railings at the top of the stairs to watch and wait. She'd seen the anger and frustration on Adam Kincaid's face the moment Aunt Margaret opened the door for him.

Paris had wanted very badly to creep downstairs and eavesdrop, but she'd been too afraid of getting caught. She'd heard the sound of muffled voices, managing to catch only a few scattered phrases. *'You can't prove a thing'* — *'no court in the country'* — *'chances of winning are slim,'* were all she could decipher.

Fifteen minutes later, Adam reappeared in the hallway, and she'd seen a look of intense relief on his face. He'd hesitated for a moment at the front door, and she'd held her breath, fearful he could hear the pounding of her heart. When he glanced up at her hiding place, she closed her eyes, praying he wouldn't see her. Several seconds passed before she ventured to look again, and she was just in time to glimpse his angry expression before he hurried from the house.

Paris had seen for herself how ill and defeated her cousin had looked after Adam's visit. Francesca spent the remainder of the weekend in her room, and though Paris tried her best to comfort her distraught cousin, she'd had little success.

Francesca's pain and bewilderment tore at Paris's young heart, and she began to feel angry and resentful toward Adam Kincaid, the man responsible for her cousin's unhappiness.

By Monday morning the tension in the house had subsided somewhat, and it was both a relief and a disappointment when Paris's parents arrived to take her home.

Once home in Florida, Paris had written Francesca every week throughout the summer months, but she'd never received a reply.

A letter from Aunt Margaret finally arrived in September, but her parents told her only snippets of its contents. Anxious to know more of what had happened to Francesca, Paris managed to commandeer the letter. She read it in its entirety before returning it to her mother's desk. From the letter, she learned Francesca had lost the baby and Aunt Margaret had sold the house in Brockton, then used the money to take her and Francesca on an extended trip to Europe.

Sadly, Aunt Margaret died later that winter while they were traveling in England. Francesca had chosen to stay on and as far as Paris knew, her cousin was living somewhere near London.

She'd never been able to forget how Francesca had suffered all those years ago. But her memories of that summer hadn't all been bad, and over the years, she'd often found herself thinking about Brockton.

When she noticed the teaching job at Brockton College advertised in the paper, she sent in her application, but hadn't held out much hope. Even after the interview, she'd been afraid to guess at her chances. When they'd called and told her the position was hers, she'd been too excited at the joy of landing her first job to have second thoughts, and once she'd moved to Brockton, there had been nothing to remind her of the past. Until now.

It was strange indeed, to find herself sitting next to the man who had been the cause of her cousin's pain and distress.

'You've been so quiet, I thought you were asleep.' Adam's voice cut through her reverie, and she felt her face grow warm under his gaze.

Paris glanced around, surprised to note they were pulling into the hospital parking lot. 'Sorry . . . it's been a hectic week.'

'You spent Christmas in Hawaii, didn't you?'

'Yes,' she answered, wondering why it seemed as if a year had passed since she'd kissed her mother and stepfather goodbye.

'We could use a little of that sunshine now,' he commented as he brought the car to a halt in a vacant space.

Adam opened his door and a blast of wind whipped a flurry of white flakes into the car. Paris reached for her door handle and climbed out into the freezing air. She turned to find Adam at her side.

With his hand at her elbow, they crossed the parking lot to the automatic doors leading into the hospital's main entrance.

Once inside, a welcome warmth wrapped itself around them. Adam kept his hand at her elbow as he ushered her toward the bank of elevators nearby.

The doors slid open, and two nurses emerged, each casting an interested glance in Adam's direction. He released his hold on Paris, and as she stepped ahead of him into the empty elevator, she found she missed the warmth, the strength, and the assurance his touch had offered. He pressed the button for the seventh floor.

They made the journey in silence and Paris found herself studying him, surreptitiously, through lowered lashes. There was no denying he was an exceedingly attractive man. She guessed him to be about thirty-six or thirty-seven, and there was about him the air of a man who knows exactly who he is, where he's going and what he wants from life.

Yet, she could see the lines of worry pinching the corners of his gold-speckled eyes. That he cared about his uncle and aunt was obvious, and Paris found this contrary to the image she'd built of him in her own mind.

Remembering his treatment of Francesca, she'd expected him to be the kind of man who cared only for himself. In fact, her encounter with him earlier in the week and his offhand dismissal of her concerns had reinforced that impression. But the concern on his face was indisputably real, and she found this strangely disturbing.

As if sensing her gaze, he glanced toward her, his amber eyes holding hers captive for an earthshattering second. In that moment her breath suddenly became trapped in her lungs, and a prickly heat chased across her nerve endings. The elevator groaned to a halt and the doors slid open. Paris blinked several times in order to break the spell she seemed to be under.

Turning from him, she hurried through the opening before the elevator doors closed once again.

'This way,' Adam said, pointing toward the corridor on the right. Rounding the corner, they came upon a nurse sitting at a desk. The sign above her read Intensive Care. Brown-haired and very attractive, the nurse gave Adam a warm smile of welcome.

'Mr. Kincaid, your uncle is doing much better this evening,' she told him. 'He's resting comfortably.'

'That's good news,' Adam said, relief in his tone. He turned to Paris and smiled, a smile that lifted the worry from his face and sent her heart galloping like a mad thing.

He turned back to the nurse. 'And my aunt, she's still here?'

'She's sitting with your uncle,' the nurse told him. 'She's been here all day. I've tried to get her to go downstairs and take a break or lie down in the visitors' lounge and rest, but she refuses.'

'We'll see what we can do,' Adam said. Indicating for Paris to follow him, he moved past the desk and down the corridor, stopping at the second door. He tapped gently, then pushed it open.

Lillian Boone, looking pale and very tired, rose from the chair by her husband's bedside and moved into her nephew's open arms.

'Adam, darling. I'm so glad you're here,' Lillian embraced Adam, who held her gently for several moments.

'Come now, Lillian, don't,' Adam chastised in a kind tone. 'You don't want George to wake and see you with tears in your eyes.' He glanced at the sleeping figure on the bed. 'I've brought you a visitor,' he went on, turning to where Paris stood behind him.

'Paris, my dear! How lovely of you to come,' Lillian said, immediately moving past Adam to embrace Paris.

'How are you?' Paris asked, as she pulled away to hold the older woman's hands in her own.

'I'm fine . . . A little tired, but all right. My poor George — for him, it's been terrible,' Lillian told her. 'He's through the worst now . . . and I thank God for that.'

'I'll sit with George for a while,' Adam said. 'Why don't you and Paris go down to the cafeteria and grab a bite to eat.'

Lillian was about to protest, but Paris quickly intervened. 'It'll do you good to take a little walk, Lillian,' she coaxed. 'You know you need a break.' She eased her toward the door.

'You're right,' Lillian agreed. But it was with obvious reluctance that she let Paris lead her from the room.

Once out in the corridor, they slowly made their way to the elevators.

'I'm really not very hungry,' Lillian said as they entered the cafeteria a few minutes later.

'How about a muffin and a cup of hot chocolate?' Paris suggested, as she took a tray from the stack on the counter.

After paying the cashier, Paris carried

the tray to an empty table and they sat down. In less than ten minutes the muffin and warm milk, were gone, and Paris noted with satisfaction that Lillian's color was much improved.

'Thank you,' Lillian said, reaching over to pat Paris's hand. 'I do feel much better now. It was so kind of you to come to the hospital,' she added, a smile touching her features. 'I'd like to go back upstairs now. George might wake up — ' She broke off and tears filled her eyes.

Paris reached across the table and covered Lillian's hand with hers. 'George is going to be just fine,' she said, her heart going out to the older woman.

'I know. But . . . ' Lillian swallowed but didn't go on.

'It's all right,' Paris said softly.

'I tried to tell him months ago that he should slow down. But he wouldn't listen to me.' Lillian sniffed and blinked away tears. She shook her head and smiled before continuing. 'I know there's

48

been something troubling George lately, but he wouldn't say a word. I was so pleased when Adam was appointed his assistant.'

'It must be a comfort to have him here,' Paris said.

'Indeed it is. Adam was the only candidate with both the experience and the credentials needed for the job, but George hadn't been sure the board would approve . . . '

'Why wouldn't they approve? Because he's your nephew?' Paris asked, unable to stop herself.

'No, nothing like that,' Lillian replied. 'It's ridiculous really, that something that happened such a long time ago should still have the power to hurt him.' She sighed. 'Adam worked at Brockton . . . oh . . . it must be eleven, no, twelve years ago. He was a coach then. Anyway, one of the students, a young girl — I forget her name — almost ruined his career.' There was bitterness in her tone now. 'She told a pack of lies about him.'

Lillian went on, then gave another tired sigh.

She shook her head as if to clear it. 'It still makes me angry every time I think about it.' She rose from the chair. 'But Adam's here. That's the important thing.' She smiled. 'I think I'd like to go back upstairs.'

Paris quickly moved to Lillian's side and took her arm. They began to make their way from the caféteria, and all the while a multitude of thoughts were spinning in Paris's head.

Lillian had to be talking about Francesca! Everything she'd said seemed to fit. But what had she meant when she'd said the girl told a pack of lies?

3

Adam rose from the chair by his uncle's bedside when the nurse entered.

'I'll have to ask you to leave for a few minutes, Mr. Kincaid,' she said as she approached the bed.

'Of course,' Adam replied, crossing to the door. He hesitated. 'He is going to be all right?' he asked, unable to hide the anxiety in his voice.

The nurse smiled at him reassuringly. 'He's coming along nicely, now,' she said. 'His will be a slow recovery, but he's over the worst. He'll probably sleep till morning, and at this stage, rest is the important thing.'

'Thank you,' Adam murmured with heartfelt relief. Once out in the corridor, he sagged against the wall for a fleeting moment, feeling as if a weight had been lifted from his shoulders. He heard the sound of voices, then straightened, quickly schooling his features.

Lillian and Paris rounded the corner and he was relieved to see that though she still looked tired, there was a hint of color in his aunt's face now, as well as a spark of life in her eyes.

'You look much better,' he said, moving to kiss her on the cheek.

'Has the nurse been in?' Lillian asked.

'She's there now,' Adam replied. 'Let's go to the visitors' lounge and wait until she's through.'

'All right,' Lillian said. Turning, she hooked her arm through Paris's and led her down the corridor to the lounge.

'You should go home and get some rest, or you'll end up in a hospital bed yourself,' Adam said as he held the door to the lounge open for them. The room was empty.

'I'm fine,' Lillian insisted, but Paris heard the weary note in the older woman's voice. She glanced at Adam, and seeing the look of concern on his face, knew he'd heard it too.

'What is there to go home to?' Lillian went on as she sank down with a sigh on the leather couch. 'I want to be here with George in case he wakes up and needs me.'

'Lillian, the nurse just told me a minute ago that George will probably sleep right through the night,' Adam said, a note of exasperation in his voice.

'I think I'll wait a while, though — at least until it stops snowing. I don't relish the thought of driving home in that.' Lillian pointed to the snow falling steadily past the window.

'Neither do I,' Adam said. 'Why don't you leave your car here and come with us?'

'Right now?' Lillian asked, her brow creasing into a worried frown.

'Listen,' Paris quickly cut in. 'You don't have to worry about taking me home. I'll call a cab.'

'Nonsense, my dear,' Lillian said. 'You live out on Devon Park Road, don't you?'

'Yes, but . . . '

'Well, then,' Lillian went on. 'The best solution would be for Adam to take you home first and come back for me. That way I can stay a little longer.'

'That sounds reasonable,' Adam agreed. 'As long as you stay right here and put your feet up for a while. I'm sure the nurses won't mind.'

'They'd probably give you a blanket and a pillow if you asked,' Paris suggested, sympathizing with Lillian's need to stay on at the hospital.

'I'll ask,' Adam said. Flashing Paris a look of gratitude, he hurried from the room. He returned a few minutes later, carrying a blanket and pillow.

'But, Adam . . . ' Lillian protested as her nephew placed the pillow behind her back.

'No buts,' Paris said, softening her words with a smile. 'You need to keep up your strength. If you don't rest you'll only jeopardize your own health — and that wouldn't be good for you or for George, now would it?'

'I suppose you're right,' Lillian said, as Adam eased his aunt's legs onto the couch and tucked the blanket around her.

'The nurse knows where you are, and she said she'd come and get you if George does wake up,' he assured her gently. 'So stop worrying and try to rest until I get back,' he added before kissing her cheek once more.

Lillian turned to Paris. 'Thank you for coming, my dear. I enjoyed our little chat.'

Paris smiled in response and squeezed the hand Lillian extended. 'I'll call you.'

'Please do,' Lillian replied.

As Paris followed Adam from the room, she found her thoughts drifting back to her conversation with Lillian and the remarks she'd made earlier in the caféteria. Francesca hadn't lied . . . What reason would she have had to lie? If anyone had lied it had to have been Adam. That his aunt cared a great deal for him was obvious, and no doubt she'd simply believed everything he'd told her.

'With any luck she might fall asleep,' Adam said, his words startling Paris out of her reverie.

She managed a tentative smile. 'Your aunt is quite a lady.'

'You can say that again,' Adam replied, flashing her a smile that made her heart instantly flip over. 'Thanks for your help back there,' he continued, as they reached the bank of elevators. 'You and Lillian seem to have hit it off.'

'Your aunt is an easy person to like,' Paris said, as the elevator arrived. 'When I started at the college in September, she called and invited me to lunch. She made me feel like one of the family. I'll never forget that.'

The elevator stopped at the third floor and several nurses joined them. They reached the main floor and the doors slid open once more. The wail of an ambulance siren as it approached cut through the air, and Paris shivered as Adam guided her through the busy corridor to the automatic doors.

Outside, huge white snowflakes were falling from the sky, adding another layer to the thick blanket of snow already on the ground.

'Perhaps I should stay in town for the night.' Paris said, surprised at how much snow had actually fallen since they'd entered the building an hour ago. 'I hate to take you so far out of your way — '

'No problem,' Adam assured her. He unlocked the passenger door and held it open for her.

'Thank you,' she murmured, as she settled against the luxurious upholstery.

'The main roads don't look too bad,' Adam commented when he joined her. He pulled out of the parking lot and into the street. 'I'll have you home in no time,' he added confidently.

Paris glanced at the digital clock on the bank building as they drove past. It was seven-thirty, still reasonably early, but the streets were quiet, with only a few vehicles braving the hazardous conditions.

Twenty minutes later, Adam turned the car onto Devon Park Road, and it was obvious from the absence of tire marks in the snow that no one had ventured this way since the storm began.

The trees on the right were laden with snow, and the farmer's field on the left looked like a scene from a Christmas card. Suddenly, Paris felt the car shift sideways and begin to slide across the road. Her heart leaped into her throat, and she glanced at Adam.

She saw the muscle of his jaw tighten with tension as he turned the car in the direction of the skid. Seconds later, the car slowly straightened its course.

'There must be sheer ice beneath the snow,' Adam commented, keeping his eyes on the road ahead.

Paris remained silent, watching the enormous snowflakes as they fell from the sky. Out in the open, away from the shelter of the houses and buildings, the wind was stronger, building in intensity, whipping the white flakes into a frenzy, and creating havoc with visibility. It wasn't until Adam turned into her driveway that Paris realized she'd been holding her breath. Slowly, deliberately, she released it.

She turned to her companion and saw mirrored on his face an image of her own relief. 'I've never seen a storm quite like this one,' Adam said, switching off the car's engine.

'You can't drive back in these conditions,' Paris said. 'You'd better come inside and call the hospital.'

'Thanks. That wind is quite vicious at the moment, and it's creating additional problems,' Adam observed. 'If I wait awhile, perhaps it'll die down.'

The wind proved to be troublesome indeed, making it difficult for them to open the car doors. Adam succeeded first, coming around to the passenger side to lend her a hand.

Paris could hardly get her breath as she stepped out into snow that was almost a foot deep. The wind suddenly caught at their backs, carrying them toward the house. With freezing fingers,

Paris fumbled with her keys, finally managing to unlock the front door.

Once inside, they stood in the shadows, simply trying to catch their breath. Paris reached for the light switch by the door, but to her surprise nothing happened.

'Oh, great!' she moaned.

'What's wrong?' Adam asked, his voice full of concern.

'The power's out.'

'I wondered about that,' he said. 'When I turned onto Devon Park Road, I noticed the streetlight on the corner was out.'

'There's a box of candles in the kitchen.' Dropping her purse on the floor at her feet, she slid her coat off and hung it on the hook behind the door.

'Which way?' Adam asked.

'Follow me.' Paris moved to pass in front of him, and in the shadowed darkness of the hall her body brushed against his, sending a frisson of heat spiraling through her. Her heart tripped over itself in reaction, and Paris had the strangest feeling that she'd just received a jolt of electricity. She hurried down the hallway, trying with some difficulty to stifle the sparks of awareness racing through her.

The eerie whiteness created by the snow outside gave off some light, and Paris, her heart thundering in her ears, rummaged through the drawer near the sink, looking for the candles she'd stored there in case of an emergency.

'Found them!' she said, as her fingers closed around the box. There were matches there, too, and in a matter of seconds, she lit a candle, and set it in a saucer she took from the cupboard.

'That's better,' Adam said, as the yellow flame brightened the room a little more.

'We passed the telephone — it's in the little alcove in the hall,' she told him.

'Thanks. I'd better make that call.' He didn't wait for her to light another candle, but turned and disappeared into the shadowed hall.

Alone now, Paris felt her heartbeat return to normal. She busied herself filling the kettle with water and setting it on the stove. It seemed only minutes later that Adam returned.

'I talked to the nurse at the intensive care unit, and she told me Lillian was asleep,' he said, a note of relief in his voice. 'I explained about the storm and said I was going to wait it out for a while.'

'It doesn't seem to be letting up at all,' Paris said, glancing out of the kitchen window. 'Thank goodness I have a gas stove. At least I'll be able to fix something to eat while we wait for the wind to die down.'

'That would be great,' Adam said, taking off his coat and dropping it over one of the kitchen chairs. 'How can I help?' He rubbed his hands together to warm them.

Paris hesitated. The thought of working alongside Adam in the confines of her small kitchen was suddenly something she wasn't quite ready to face. 'Perhaps you could build a fire in the living room,' she suggested. 'You'll find everything you need in the wooden box by the fireplace.'

'And your living room is . . . ?'

'Ah . . . right across the hall.' Taking another candle from the box, she lit it and held it out to him. 'You'd better take a candle with you this time.'

'Thanks,' Adam said. As he took the candle from her, their fingers touched for a fraction of a second. In that brief moment, Paris felt a tingling sensation chase along her arm, sending alarm signals to her brain.

Annoyance flickered through her at the response she couldn't seem to control. When he turned and made his way from the kitchen, she stood motionless, waiting for her heartbeat to return to normal.

What was it about Adam Kincaid that seemed to call out to her senses, to ignite emotions she'd only read about in books?

Throughout her adolescence and on through college, she'd shied away from becoming involved with, or dependent on, any man. She'd gone out on dates, and had been kissed a number of times by young men all too eager to show her all that a relationship could be, but somehow she'd never found anyone who had managed to arouse her curiosity . . . much less her passion.

She'd often thought that the memory of the pain and heartache Francesca had suffered had had something to do with her decision to never get too close to any man.

But here she was with Adam Kincaid — the man responsible for breaking Francesca's heart — and she was fighting to hold her emotions in check, fighting an attraction that seemed to grow stronger each time he came near her.

Resolutely, Paris pushed these thoughts aside, and picking up the candle from the table, she opened the door to the refrigerator.

Though the shelves were by no means full, there was enough to provide a half-way decent meal, she thought, as she surveyed the carton of milk, the eggs, the block of cheese and the ham slices she'd bought the previous evening. She'd stopped off at the corner store on her way home from the college, buying only enough to tide her over until the weekend.

'Ham and cheese omelets will have to do,' she said aloud.

'Sounds fine to me,' Adam said, as he reentered the kitchen. He flashed a smile as he crossed to where she stood.

Paris edged away from him, dismayed at the way her pulse had picked up speed the moment she'd heard his voice. Dammit! She was reacting like a lovesick teenager who'd suddenly found herself alone with the handsomest boy in class.

'You must have set the fireplace already,' he told her. 'All it needs now is a match. Why don't I get started on the omelets?' He reached for the egg carton. 'Where do you hide your bowls?'

Paris quickly located a bowl and handed it to him. Adam set it on the counter, and with accustomed ease broke several eggs into it. He reached for the old-fashioned eggbeater she kept in the handy utensil jar nearby, and like a man familiar with such devices, he set to work.

Paris busied herself grating the cheese and dicing the ham. To her surprise, they worked together well, and soon an appetizing aroma filled the kitchen, making her mouth water.

She set two places at the table and in no time at all, they sat down to eat. The candles flickering in the center of the kitchen table seemed to create a romantic atmosphere, an atmosphere Paris found difficult to ignore.

Throughout the meal, their conversation centered around food. Their discussion ranged from different styles of cooking to the use of various spices. Paris was impressed by his knowledge and she'd quickly realized that for him, cooking was a form of relaxation, a way to ease tensions.

'That was delicious,' Adam said, cleaning the last morsel from his plate.

Paris met his gaze across the table and tried to ignore the way her pulse kicked into gear. Deliberately she turned her eyes toward the window. 'Doesn't look much like the weather's improving,' she commented. She rose and gathered the dishes, then set them in the sink.

'I think I'll call the local radio station and find out if the weather conditions are expected to improve in the next little while.'

'Go ahead. I'll pour the coffee and take it through to the living room,' she said turning to the stove.

'Shall I put a match to the fire now?' he asked, stopping in the doorway.

'Yes, thanks,' Paris answered, before turning back to the sink. She heard the kitchen door swing shut and she stood for several moments trying to sort out her feelings.

Her initial antagonism, the anger and resentment she'd felt for Adam Kincaid earlier that week, seemed to have vanished — at least for the time being. But she found it difficult to come to terms with the fact that during the past few hours she'd come very close to liking him. She remembered the concern and love he'd shown his aunt, and she found herself admiring the way he seemed to be taking this latest development in stride.

Thoughtfully, she poured coffee into two mugs and set them on a tray. She added teaspoons, a china cream pitcher and matching sugar bowl, and taking a deep breath, she headed for the living room.

She glanced at Adam standing at the phone, and from the grim expression on his face, she sensed the information he was being given wasn't in the least encouraging.

He hung up and joined her in the living room. Crossing to the armchair near the fire, he sat down. 'The weatherman at the radio station told me the police are advising motorists to stay off the roads tonight, unless it's an emergency. Road crews are out plowing and sanding, but conditions are very bad. The good news is that the storm is supposed to blow itself out by midnight,' he went on. 'Thanks,' he added, as he accepted a coffee mug from the tray she held out to him.

'What about your aunt?' Paris asked, setting the tray beside the candle on the mahogany table in front of the fire.

'I'll call the hospital again in a minute,' Adam said. He watched her add cream to her coffee, then sit down on the three-seater Chesterfield directly opposite the fireplace. 'I'm sorry about this,' he continued. 'But it looks like you're stuck with a house guest for the night.'

'That's all right,' Paris assured him, quickly. 'The storm wasn't your fault. You should have let me call for that taxi. If my car had started like it was supposed to, you wouldn't be stranded here,' she added.

As she took another sip of coffee, the realization that Adam would be spending the night under the same roof began to register in her brain.

The house only had one bedroom. She would have to make up a bed for him here, on the couch. Suddenly, an image of Adam, his long lean body stretched out beside her, filled her mind. Her pulse jerked into action, sending urgent and conflicting messages to every cell, stirring to life sensations that were new and bewildering.

What on earth was the matter with her? She jumped to her feet, almost spilling the contents of her mug.

'Is something wrong?' Adam asked, effectively cutting into her wayward thoughts.

'No, nothing,' she replied, glad of the flickering flames that helped to hide the blush rising in her cheeks. She put her mug on the tray and knelt before the fire, where she began to poke at the burning logs, sending a shower of sparks up the chimney.

'I appreciate the fact that you seem to be taking all this in stride,' Adam said. 'Especially since we didn't exactly see eye to eye on our first meeting.'

Paris shrugged her shoulders. 'It wouldn't be very neighborly of me not to offer you refuge for the night, when I'm the reason you're here in the first place,' she said, keeping her eyes averted.

'I'd like to apologize for being so abrupt with you that day. My only excuse is that you caught me at a bad moment,' he said.

Paris blinked twice, taken aback as much by the apology as by the sincerity in his voice.

'You had a lot on your mind,' she said, surprised that she should feel sympathy and understanding now, when at the time she'd been so angry.

Adam put his elbows on his knees and leaning forward, he stared into the flames. 'I just hope George is back on his feet soon,' he said. 'The fact that I'm acting athletic director isn't sitting too well with a couple of the board members . . . '

Paris heard the trace of bitterness in his tone. 'But why would they object?' she asked, unable to stop herself.

His head came around and as their glances collided, she found herself wishing she hadn't asked. His amber eyes looked dangerously hard and stubbornly unyielding, and she glimpsed a look of anger in their depths — anger and something more she couldn't quite define.

'I'm sorry. It's really none of my business — ' Paris hurriedly withdrew her question.

'You're right, it isn't,' he said, and Paris flinched at the hard edge of steel in his voice. 'I'm sorry,' he said, immediately contrite. 'Perhaps you'll understand my frustration when I tell you that their objection stems from an incident that happened here at the college more than twelve years ago.' He rose abruptly and ran a hand through his hair. 'I'd better give the hospital a call . . . '

With that he turned away, but not before Paris saw a look of pain and regret cross his features.

4

Paris watched in silence as Adam left the living room. Thoughtfully, she picked up the tray and carried it through to the kitchen.

She heard the low murmur of his voice as she cleared the tray and set about using the remaining hot water in the kettle to wash the dishes they'd used.

Her thoughts, as she added detergent to the water, were centered around Adam and the bitter words he'd spoken a few minutes ago. After hearing Lillian's comments in the caféteria and now Adam's own mention of an incident twelve years ago, Paris felt totally confused.

Was it possible there was more to what she knew and understood of what had happened? She was sure the incident they'd both referred to had been the one involving Francesca. But she couldn't understand his anger or bitterness. If the incident had had repercussions for Adam, they'd been minor compared to what Francesca had been through — she'd been the one who had suffered, the one whose life had been ruined.

'Where's the towel? I'll dry.' Adam's voice startled Paris, causing the mug in her hands to slip from her fingers into the suds:

'There's not enough to worry about,' Paris said, feeling her pulse pick up speed. She glanced at Adam standing at the counter nearby, tea towel in his hands. Their eyes met for a brief second, and not for the first time Paris found herself drawn to the raw masculinity that seemed to emanate from him.

Her skin tingled with awareness and she quickly focused her attention on the bubbles in the sink, finding the errant mug. She kept her head averted, hoping Adam wouldn't notice the blush of

75

color she knew was staining her cheeks.

'Did you talk to your aunt?' she asked, her voice slightly uneven as she set the mug on the draining board.

'No, she's still asleep,' Adam replied, deftly drying the plates they'd used. 'I told the nurse not to wake her. Thanks to the storm, Lillian isn't the only visitor stranded at the hospital for the night. If we hadn't left when we did, we would have had to spend the night there, too.'

Paris said nothing, not sure whether or not to be glad they were here instead of at the hospital. Adam Kincaid was an attractive, dynamic man, a fact she was growing increasingly aware of with each minute that passed. His nearness was playing havoc with her senses and the thought of him spending the night under the same roof was creating a tension inside her she found strangely disturbing.

'Look!' Adam leaned toward her, gazing out of the window above the sink.

Paris followed his gaze and instantly saw the shadowy figure of an animal running across the backyard. It was larger than a cat and it seemed to shamble along rather awkwardly.

'It's Charlie, the raccoon,' she said, recognizing the creature that had appeared at her back door a number of times in the past month. 'There's a family of them in the woods. They come scrounging for scraps every now and then.' She smiled and turned to Adam to discover his face was only inches from hers.

'Charlie,' he said, amusement twinkling in his eyes. 'Do you feed them?' he asked, his breath fanning her face, sending shivers of both alarm and excitement racing through her.

'Sometimes,' she said, a trifle breathlessly before turning away, determined to put some distance between herself and Adam. Her heart was pounding in her ears and she willed it to slow down as she crossed to the table. She was angry with herself, wishing suddenly they had been stranded at the hospital instead of here in this intimate setting. She picked up the salt and pepper shakers from the table, but her fingers were wet and she was having trouble holding on to them.

'Give me those, before you drop them,' he said, reaching out to her, the dish towel in his hands. He cupped her hands in his and held on for several long seconds. Paris could feel his warmth, his strength slowly seeping into her.

What she'd been attempting to avoid — physical contact — had happened in spite of her efforts, and the impact was more heady than drinking a glass of champagne.

She lifted her head and found herself staring into his honey-gold eyes. Her heart shuddered to a halt, then tripped over itself as it picked up speed once more. What would it be like to be kissed by him? she wondered, as she tried to fight the unfamiliar wave of longing washing over her.

All she had to do was close the gap between them and she'd find out. The temptation was almost more than she could resist.

'You have the most incredible eyes,' he said, his voice as soft as a caress.

Her legs felt weak and her body swayed toward his, but suddenly an image of Francesca's tearstained face flashed into her mind and Paris stiffened, instantly withdrawing both physically and mentally. What on earth was she doing? Adam Kincaid was the man responsible for all the pain and grief her cousin had gone through. And she would do well to remember that.

'I'd better see if I can find some blankets and a pillow for you,' Paris said, wrenching her hands away and placing the salt and pepper shakers on the ledge over the sink. Inside she was shaking, fighting with emotions she didn't want to feel. 'You'll be warm by the fire, and the couch is quite comfortable,' she rambled on as she crossed to the door.

'That's fine,' he answered, but she was already gone.

* * *

'What was that all about, I wonder?' Adam said softly to himself as he drew a hand through his hair and stared at the door Paris had just exited.

For a fleeting moment he'd been sure he'd seen an invitation in her lovely green eyes and the sweet stab of desire it elicited had surprised him. A warmth had begun to unfurl inside him and he'd been more than a little curious to discover if the look of innocence she had about her was real or simply a façade.

Then suddenly the air had turned as chilly as the wind outside and she'd bolted like a scared rabbit. Adam shook his head. It was probably just as well, he thought. He had enough on his mind right now without involving himself with Paris Ford. But he had to admit that she had aroused his interest as no

80

woman had in a long time.

It was obvious that she wasn't in the habit of entertaining men, at least not overnight, and to his surprise he felt intensely glad about that. And on reflection her frightened reaction seemed to confirm that the air of innocence surrounding her was indeed real. As this thought settled over him, he felt something stir deep inside him, a forgotten emotion he couldn't define.

He heard a noise in the hall, and tossing the tea towel on the counter, he made his way from the room.

Paris dropped the blankets and pillow on the armchair next to the fireplace and turned to find Adam watching her from the doorway.

'Will that be enough?' she asked. 'I have more blankets upstairs . . . '

'Thanks, but that should suffice,' he said moving to stand behind the couch.

'Then, I'll bid you good-night,' Paris said, obviously anxious to make her escape. She stopped in the doorway and turned to him once more. 'Oh, the bathroom is straight ahead at the top of the stairs. I put out fresh towels and a toothbrush . . . I'm afraid I don't have a razor.' Her face reddened under his steady gaze.

Adam smiled. 'Thanks, I'll manage,' he said as he reached for the blankets.

★ ★ ★

Paris crossed to the kitchen to retrieve the candle that had almost burned down. She glanced at the mugs still sitting on the counter and was tempted for a moment to finish the job she'd started, but a sound from across the hall made her change her mind. She'd clear them away in the morning, she decided, as she hurried toward the stairs.

She undressed in the bathroom, listening all the while for the sound of Adam's footsteps on the stairs. Only when she was safely in her own room did she begin to relax.

It had been an eventful evening, and

as she lay staring at the ceiling, she tried to tell herself her reactions to Adam were simply due to her own lack of experience with men. Not that she hadn't dated — she had. But during high school and on into college she'd been concerned about her education, and unlike some of the girls she'd known, she'd been more interested in achieving good grades and attaining the goals she'd set for herself, than worrying about having or not having a boyfriend.

While at college she'd enjoyed going to parties with a group of friends, and she'd had an occasional date, but after seeing several of her girlfriends grow despondent after the breakup of a relationship, she'd made a point of keeping men at a safe distance, of never letting her guard down. And always at the back of her mind was the memory of the pain and heartache Francesca had suffered at the hands of Adam Kincaid.

Anger stirred to life inside her and

she welcomed the emotion, which effectively dispelled the new and unwanted emotions Adam's presence aroused in her.

They worked at the same college and it was inevitable that they would see each other from time to time. Their relationship was purely a professional one and, as she drifted off to sleep, she resolved to keep that firmly in mind.

* * *

Paris rolled over and pulling the pillow into her arms, hugged it to her. Suddenly the sound of a door closing and footsteps on the stairs brought her instantly awake. She sat up and listened for a moment, hearing the faint creak of the kitchen door as it was opened.

Who? What? Fear sent the adrenaline pumping through her veins until the memory of the previous evening returned. Adam! Of course, it had to be. She released the breath she'd been holding and sank back against the pillows, annoyed at her own foolishness.

She pushed the covers aside, crossing to the window to gaze out at the snow. The white blanket seemed to stretch endlessly before her, with only trees and fences breaking up the landscape. The world looked incredibly peaceful, the entire scene like a work of art painted on canvas.

Suddenly she had an urge to race downstairs, out into the snow and make snow angels like she'd done numerous times as a child. She squashed the impulse and shaking her head, she smiled at the childish notion.

She drew a deep breath, and with it the aroma of freshly brewed coffee reached her. She turned from the window and grabbing her dressing gown from the hook on the back of her bedroom door, she headed for the bathroom.

She washed her face, brushed her teeth and ran a comb through her blond hair, realizing as she did that the light was on — electricity had been restored. She emerged into the hall and glanced at her bedroom, trying to decide whether or not to dress first, but the enticing smell of coffee pulled her down the stairs and into the kitchen.

Adam stood at the sink with his back to her. He'd rolled up his shirtsleeves and as he turned, she saw the play of muscles ripple across his back.

'Good morning,' he said, his glance quickly traveling the length of her, making Paris wish she had taken the time to return to her bedroom to dress.

'Good morning,' she managed, as she tugged self-consciously at the belt of her housecoat. His hair was slightly tousled and there was the hint of stubble on his jawline, but it served to add another dimension to what she could only describe as latent sex appeal.

'I made a pot of coffee. I hope you don't mind,' he said, and followed his words with a warm smile that sent her heart flip-flopping in response.

'Why would I mind?' she replied. He'd already done more for her in the last twenty-four hours than any man she'd ever known.

She crossed to the cupboard to retrieve a mug, and noticed as she did that the sink was clean and the dishes she'd left rather hurriedly the previous night had been dried and put away. Was there no end to this man's thoughtfulness? she wondered as she filled a mug with coffee.

'Do you like French toast?' she heard him ask.

She turned. 'Yes . . . but . . . '

'Good,' he cut in, his smile widening as he moved to the stove. 'These won't take a minute,' he told her, as he dipped bread into the bowl he was holding.

The table was already set for two and Paris crossed to it and sat down. Ever since she'd started attending college she'd shared accommodations or lived alone, and it was a novelty indeed to have someone, and especially a man, cook for her. As she watched him drop the bread into the frying pan, she found herself thinking that she could happily get used to waking up to this every morning.

Dear heaven! What on earth was she thinking about, she chided herself. She didn't want to like Adam Kincaid. Just because he was being both thoughtful and considerate didn't mean she had to succumb to his charm. Francesca had fallen for his easy charm and he'd proceeded to break her heart. Paris was not about to make the same mistake.

'The storm blew itself out about midnight,' Adam said, breaking into her thoughts. 'I called the radio station a little while ago and was told that the road crews will have the main highways cleared soon, then I'll get out of your way.'

'Did you call the hospital?' Paris asked, taking a sip of coffee, ignoring the tiny corner of her mind that was saying she didn't want him to leave.

'Yes. I talked to Lillian. She spent a restful night, by the sound of things. George did, too. I told her I'd stop by

88

the hospital and pick her up on my way home.'

'Could you drop me off at Gibson's Garage? I'll get someone to drive over to the college to take a look at my car.'

'No problem,' he said easily. 'Here, try this,' he added as he put a plate with two slices of nicely browned French toast in front of her.

★ ★ ★

Two hours later, Adam pulled his car up to the curb opposite Gibson's Garage.

'Thanks for the ride,' Paris said as she reached for the door handle.

'Thanks for your hospitality,' Adam replied. 'I hope you'll let me repay you by taking you out to dinner sometime soon.'

Paris hesitated. Part of her longed to say yes, but she stifled the impulse. 'It's really not necessary,' she said, her tone slightly stilted.

'Please, I insist,' he said.

She glanced at him and saw only sincerity in his eyes, but she clung to her resolve, afraid that if she agreed to go out with him she would be nothing short of a traitor.

'Thank you, but no,' she said firmly, and immediately felt a pang of regret when she saw the look of disappointment that came into his eyes.

'Then I'll just have to think of another way to show my appreciation,' he said softly, and followed his words with a smile that sent her heart racing.

Slightly flustered now, Paris pushed the car door open and stepped out onto the snow-covered sidewalk. As she watched him drive away, she wondered why she felt as if she were being torn in two.

She tried to tell herself that Adam had invited her to dinner out of courtesy and nothing more, and that it was unlikely in view of her refusal that he would pursue the matter. But for the remainder of the weekend, Paris found his image constantly invading her thoughts.

Each time she walked into the kitchen, she found herself remembering how he'd looked standing at the stove cooking breakfast for her. She was being utterly foolish and she knew it, but she couldn't help wishing that the Adam Kincaid she'd come to like wasn't the same man who'd ruthlessly trampled over her cousin's feelings all those years ago.

By Monday morning, Paris had nearly convinced herself that she had simply overreacted to the situation of having to spend the night under the same roof as Adam Kincaid.

The temperature had risen several degrees and the snow on the roadsides was already turning to slush as she drove to the college. She'd had her car towed to Gibson's Garage to be checked over and she was driving a small Japanese model they'd loaned her.

As she pulled into the parking lot, she noticed Adam's car parked where it had been the night he'd driven her home. It was doubtful she'd see him during the course of her day, and with this thought came a stab of disappointment.

She shook her head in annoyance and resolutely pushed all thoughts of Adam Kincaid from her mind as she crossed to the main building.

When she reached her classroom and heard the commotion inside, she turned her attention to the day ahead and to the job she'd been hired to do.

Her second period that morning was the senior class, three of whom were members of the basketball team. Throughout her hour-long lecture, she was conscious of the fact that none of the three team members was taking notes, and none of them bothered to heed her instruction to turn to a specific page in the novel she was discussing.

Much as she tried to ignore it, she was aware of a certain tension in the air.

'One more thing before the bell rings,' Paris said, keeping her tone even. 'Could Jason French, Rick Diamond and Barry Kralic please stay behind for a few minutes? Thank you. That's all for today. Remember, this assignment is due in two weeks.'

The bell rang just as she finished and Paris gathered her papers together as she waited for the other students to file out.

The three young men lounged lazily in their seats and when the door at last closed, leaving her alone with the three students, Paris drew a deep, steadying breath as she faced them.

'I know all three of you are aware that your marks in English are well below what is expected and accepted by this college. The examination you wrote before Christmas was a total disaster, but I know you had a heavy schedule, with basketball practices, weight-training, as well as home and away games.

'However, I don't need to remind you that it's an internal college rule here at Brockton that a student must acquire a passing grade each term, and not merely a passing grade for the whole year.'

'Yeah, so what!' Jason French said insolently as he dropped his feet noisily onto the floor and slowly stood up.

'Look!' Paris said, as a shiver of apprehension chased down her spine. 'I'm really not the enemy here. All I'm concerned about is that you fulfill the college requirements in order to graduate, and passing English every term is a requirement.'

'She's not the enemy! Did you hear that, guys?' Jason laughed as he glanced at his two friends, who stood up and started to move toward the front of the class.

'I've come up with a compromise,' Paris quickly went on. 'I'm going to give you an additional assignment with the stipulation that you hand it in by three o'clock this Friday. And if you receive a passing grade for this assignment, I'll reconsider taking steps to suspend you from the basketball team.' She dropped her gaze and rummaged through the papers in her briefcase for the assignment she'd prepared the day before.

'Well, isn't that generous.' Jason French's tone was heavy with sarcasm as the three young men gradually moved in closer.

Paris looked up and kept her smile in place, all the while fighting the feeling of fear slowly taking hold.

'Yeah! We really appreciate this, Miss Ford,' Barry Kralic echoed, his tone threaded with laughter.

'But Mrs. Wilkinson never gave us extra assignments,' Rich Diamond moaned.

'I'm not Mrs. Wilkinson,' Paris said, recognizing the name of the teacher she'd replaced. 'Different teachers have different methods,' she added, trying to keep her tone even.

'She was a sweet old lady, Mrs. Wilkinson,' Jason continued. 'She was always so nice to us. She never gave us homework at all. We were her favorites, weren't we, guys? It's too bad she decided to retire early.'

Paris felt her smile slipping away. It wasn't difficult to read between the lines. Though she had no proof, Paris felt sure that these three young men had successfully intimidated Mrs. Wilkinson. Now they were trying the same tactics on her.

With fresh resolve summoned by the anger now coursing through her, Paris held out the papers. 'Here you are, gentlemen.'

No one moved, and the air was suddenly electric with tension. All Paris could hear was the sound of her heart hammering against her rib cage.

A loud knock on the door startled them and Paris glanced at the new-comer with relief. But her relief was short-lived when she saw Neil Pavan standing in the open doorway.

'Excuse me, Miss Ford, but Professor Chancellor is waiting for you in your office,' Neil said, making no move to join the threesome.

Paris felt the tension inside her ease fractionally. Dropping the papers on the desk in front of her, she gathered up her purse. Then, closing the lid of her briefcase, she turned and smiled at Neil as she walked toward the door.

'Thank you, Neil,' she said as she came to a halt in the doorway. 'Oh, and don't forget,' she said, turning back now to face the three young men. 'I'd like those handed in by Friday afternoon.'

5

Neil was silent as he walked with Paris along the hallway. They turned a corner and arrived at the stairway leading up to the second floor, where her office was located.

'Professor Chancellor isn't in your office, Miss Ford,' said Neil coming to a halt at the foot of the stairs. 'I made that up . . . '

'I don't understand,' Paris replied, frowning at him.

'I came to your classroom to talk to you,' he hurried on. 'And when I glanced through the window in the door . . . well, it looked like those guys were giving you a rough time . . . '

'I appreciate your concern, Neil, but there really wasn't a problem,' Paris said evenly, unwilling to admit that for a fleeting moment back in the class-room, she had been frightened. Now that she was no longer alone with the three senior students, she wasn't sure whether or not her imagination had been working overtime. 'What did you want to see me about?' she asked, deliberately pushing aside thoughts of Jason French and his friends.

'My English mark,' said Neil hesitatingly. 'I wanted to ask if there was something I could do . . . a retest maybe, something to bring my grade up . . . '

Paris smiled. 'That's what I was talking to those students about,' she said, glancing back down the hall.

'You were?' Neil said in disbelief.

'Yes. I thought about it all weekend and decided to give those of you whose marks were low on that last examination a chance to improve your grade. If you're willing to complete an extra assignment, I'm willing to add the mark to your present grade.'

'You are? That's great!' Neil said, a smile lighting up his features.

'I was going to ask you and the other

two students to see me after class this afternoon, but if you want to come to my office now, I'll give you the assignments and you can hand them out for me,' she told him, as she headed up the stairs.

'I really appreciate this, and so will the other guys,' Neil said a few minutes later as he took the sheets of paper she held out to him.

'I want a passing grade, if not better,' she cautioned. 'And they have to be handed in by three o'clock on Friday.'

'No problem,' Neil assured her. 'Thanks again,' he added, then stopped in the doorway. 'Oh . . . Miss Ford, I was just wondering if you were going to the basketball game tonight. We're playing the Brentwood Hawks, a team from Portland, and they're always tough to beat.'

'Actually I was thinking about going. Sounds like it might be quite an exciting game,' she said, feeling caught up in his enthusiasm. 'It starts at eight, doesn't it?'

'Right,' he replied. 'See you there,' he added and was gone.

Paris sank back in her swivel chair and smiled. She hadn't been to a basketball game in ages and she was more than a little curious to see how the players performed. Besides, it wouldn't hurt to show the team that she did support their efforts.

After the idea of giving the players an extra assignment had come to mind, she'd spent the best part of Sunday afternoon choosing an appropriate topic. She'd thought doing an extra assignment was a fair and reasonable compromise, and hoped the six students in question would agree. The fact that Jason French and his two friends hadn't rejected her suggestion outright was a positive sign, but she could still recall that feeling of tension just before Neil knocked on the door. All she could do now was wait until the deadline and hope she wouldn't have to take further action.

Neil, at least, seemed genuinely

pleased with her decision. Up until the term examination two weeks before Christmas, his assignments had always been handed in on time. And while his marks were borderline, his work had showed promise. The fact that he'd done as poorly as he had in the exam had surprised her — it was as if he hadn't even bothered to try.

Paris opened her briefcase and withdrew the brown lunch bag she'd stowed there. Thoughtfully, she unwrapped the egg-salad sandwich she'd made that morning.

As she munched on her sandwich, she decided to walk over to the gymnasium after lunch and talk to Stuart Unger, the coach. Though he hadn't been in the least interested or cooperative when she'd approached him before Christmas to talk about the six students, she felt she should explain her position once more.

She knew and understood the importance of athletics and sports in any college, but she recognized, too, that the chances of every player going on to play professionally was slim indeed.

Competition in the field of sports was very strong throughout the country, and on top of that was the constant threat of injury, which could all too easily put an end to a potential career.

Paris believed it was her job to ensure that each student, athlete or otherwise, left the college with a degree in his hands and a chance for the future.

She finished the sandwich and tossed the plastic wrap into the garbage can by her desk before reaching for the crisp red apple that was her dessert.

Ten minutes later, she made her way from the office and across campus to the gymnasium. As she approached the gym, she rehearsed in her head what she would tell the coach. Stuart Unger's office was located on the mezzanine floor, and as she climbed the stairs, she wondered momentarily if she should have called first and made an appointment.

The door to his office was open and

he was seated behind the desk, busily using a calculator and writing figures on a notepad. At her knock he glanced up, and a look of surprise flashed across his features before he quickly composed himself. He closed the file in front of him and dropped it into a tray on his desk.

'Well, well,' he said, and the speculative gleam she could see in his eyes set her teeth on edge. 'Come in!' Tilting back his chair, he put his feet up on the desk and clasped his hands behind his head, then let his glance slide over her in a way that made her feel decidedly uncomfortable. 'To what do I owe the pleasure?' he drawled.

'Can you spare a few minutes?' she asked, keeping her tone light, while inside she could feel the tension mounting.

'For you, anything,' came the quick reply, and the smile that followed made her skin crawl. 'Sit down,' he said, nodding toward the chair opposite.

'Thank you,' she replied, already

wishing she'd used the telephone to convey her news instead of paying him a visit.

She glanced at him as she sat down, noting that his hair was beginning to recede. She guessed his age to be around forty-five, and though quite muscular looking in build, he appeared now to be more than a little overweight. The jogging suit he wore stretched over his frame in a way that was distinctly unappealing, but Paris had the impression Stuart Unger considered himself attractive. She knew very little about him other than that he had recently been divorced.

'What can I do for you?' he asked, and again the question was accompanied by a smile that was all invitation.

Paris controlled the shiver of distaste that chased along her nerve endings. 'I've come to talk about your basketball players,' she said.

His smile disappeared and his eyes narrowed, and she saw his mouth twitch nervously. Dropping his feet onto the floor, he leaned toward her. 'What about them?' he asked guardedly.

'As I explained to you before Christmas, six players failed to achieve a passing grade for the term and according to the rules they should automatically be suspended from the team . . .'

'Now just a minute,' Stuart Unger snarled, dislike for her evident on his face. 'I've been the basketball coach at this college for four years and I've never had a problem like this before. Do you realize how important this team is to the college? We're in contention for the divisional championship this year and I plan to win that championship and take my team all the way to the nationals. Nothing and no one is going to stop me.' His eyes bored into hers and not for the first time that day, Paris sensed a threat in the air.

'Look, I'm not out to stop the team from winning the championship.' Paris quickly tried to reassure him. 'But surely you don't expect me to ignore the rules and policies of the college?'

'I don't give a monkey's uncle about the rules you're talking about,' Stuart Unger said scornfully. 'If you suspend just one of those players, you're going to jeopardize the team's chances. I've worked too hard and too long to let everything slip away now.' He slammed his fist on the desk and leaned across it, his face reddening, perspiration breaking out on his forehead. 'We have to win. There's a lot more at stake here ... ' He broke off abruptly, cursing under his breath as he rose from the chair.

Paris felt a shiver of alarm chase across her skin. She hadn't expected this explosive reaction, and she couldn't help feeling that his anger seemed somehow out of proportion to the problem. She swallowed nervously, fighting the urge to leave. 'If you'll listen to me for a minute, I'll tell you what I've decided to do,' she said, filling the tense silence.

Stuart Unger turned and glared at

her for a long moment, his anger almost palpable. Then he crossed his arms in front of his chest waiting for her to continue.

Paris took a deep breath. 'I hear what you're saying,' she said evenly, 'and believe me I do know what it would mean to the college to win a divisional championship,' she went on. 'But I can't compromise my principles or the principles of the college. These students aren't here just for the athletic program, they're here to get an education . . . earn a degree, and it's my job to see that they reach that goal.' A hint of exasperation entered her voice. 'I've offered the students a compromise. If they complete an additional assignment and hand it in by the deadline I've set, and if the work is completed to my satisfaction, they'll be off the hook — at least for this term.'

'An extra assignment . . . ' said Unger, shaking his head.

'You don't approve?' Paris couldn't hide her surprise.

'Look, lady!' Unger said, coming around the desk. 'Tonight's game and the next two on the team's schedule are critical ones. I can't afford to be without any of my players,' he said bitingly. 'Why don't you do us both a favor and just give those guys a passing grade?'

Paris stood, too, anger and outrage welling up inside her. 'I'm afraid I can't do that,' she said, fighting to maintain her control.

'Why not? It won't make a bit of difference in the long run,' Unger replied.

'Why do you say that?' she asked.

Unger laughed, and yet Paris detected a hint of anxiety in the sound. 'If you think Adam Kincaid will agree to suspend those players, you've got a lot to learn.'

'What makes you think he won't?' Paris asked angrily.

'Because he's an old friend of mine. We coached basketball together in a college back east. He knows exactly what the divisional championship will mean to the players and to the college. Winning a berth to the national championships is what's important. Nothing else matters. He won't do anything that will jeopardize the team's chances. Believe me, Adam won't give a hoot whether the players have passed English or not.'

Unger's words and the confidence with which he spoke filled her with dismay, but she refused to let him see her reaction.

'My terms still stand,' she told him calmly. 'If those six students complete the assignment to my satisfaction, the problem will be resolved, and there won't be any need for me to take further action.'

Unger's cold blue eyes bored into hers for a long moment, but Paris held her ground, refusing to back down. Unger was the first to look away. Dropping his gaze, he ran a hand around the collar of his sweat-shirt in a gesture that spoke of nervousness.

'You do what you have to do,' he said softly. 'And I'll do what I have to do.'

Paris heard the unmistakable threat in his voice, and a shudder ran through her. Suddenly the sound of footsteps broke the tension and they both turned. When Adam came into view, Paris felt her heart leap at the sight of him. Dressed in a brown tweed jacket, pale beige shirt and brown pants, he looked incredibly handsome and every inch a professional.

'Am I interrupting something?' he asked, his glance shifting from one to the other.

'No way, man. Come in! Come in.' Unger said, a smile creasing his features now. 'It's about time you came by to see me,' he scolded, as he practically shoved Paris out of his way.

Paris watched the men as they greeted each other. The hand shaking and back slapping that ensued showed her all too clearly that a friendship existed between them.

'You'll have to excuse our bad

manners,' Adam said, turning to Paris. 'But with all that's been happening lately, this is the first time I've had a minute to stop by and say 'hello.''

'I quite understand,' Paris said, but before she could take her leave of them Adam turned back to Unger.

'From what I hear you're doing a great job with the basketball team this year,' Adam said.

'They're a great bunch of guys,' Unger replied.

'What are the chances? Is the team going to go all the way?' Adam asked.

'They're going to win, all right. You can bet your boots on that,' Unger said, as he flashed a triumphant glance at Paris.

'I like your attitude,' Adam said with a smile. 'And winning the divisional championship would certainly give the college a much needed boost. Let's face it, winning is what it's all about,' Adam added, his smile widening to encompass Paris.

With every word Adam uttered, Paris

felt her dismay deepening. 'If you'll excuse me, I have to get back to work,' she said coolly. Without waiting for a reply, she crossed to the door and hurried down the stairs.

As Paris made her way back to her office, she found her thoughts dwelling on her confrontation with Unger. Though she'd sensed a certain nervousness and anxiety in him when she'd first arrived, he'd angrily dismissed her suggestion of a compromise.

Listening to Unger's angry words just before Adam arrived, she'd thought he was bluffing, refusing to believe that the administration would condone handing out passing grades to students simply because of their athletic ability. Even when he'd suggested that Adam agreed with and supported his philosophy, that winning was all that mattered, she hadn't believed him.

But the conversation she'd heard between the two men had confirmed what Unger had told her — that as far as they were concerned, winning was everything.

Paris shook her head in disbelief. It couldn't be true? Could it? To her surprise, she discovered that she didn't want to believe Adam shared this philosophy. But at the back of her mind was the memory of how Adam had treated Francesca twelve years ago.

Hadn't he come out the winner there? And at what cost to Francesca?

Paris unlocked the door to her office, slipped off her coat, and dropped it over a chair. She sat down at her desk and propped her head on her hands before combing her fingers through her hair.

Twelve years ago she hadn't fully understood all that had happened, but she'd never been able to erase the pain and devastation she'd seen on Francesca's face the day Adam walked out of the house.

Over a period of time, she'd slowly filled in the blanks herself, reaching the conclusion that Adam had run rough-shod over her cousin with a total lack of concern for the emotional toll he'd extracted.

He'd won! But his methods, in her opinion, had been despicable. And indeed, Adam Kincaid was still the kind of man who lived by his own set of rules.

After her last class of the day, Paris drove to Gibson's Garage to pick up her car. The temperature had dropped and the air was decidedly chilly as she pulled into the garage and stepped out. Turning up the collar of her coat, she crossed to the office and once inside, wrinkled up her nose at the smell of gasoline and oil that permeated the place. The mechanic who'd been working in the workshop area at the rear of the building appeared, wiping his hands on an oily rag.

'What was wrong with my car?' Paris asked when he joined her.

'Well, miss, it's my guess somebody tampered with it,' he replied as he walked around the other side of the desk.

'Tampered with it? What on earth do you mean?'

'Exactly what I said,' the mechanic told her, tossing the rag into a bin nearby. 'The wires leading to the solenoid had been cut.'

'Cut? But surely there's some mistake,' Paris said, struggling now with the implications of what he was saying.

'No mistake, miss. It was cut clean through, and that kind of thing doesn't happen by accident.'

'But who — '

'Aren't you a new teacher at the college?' he interrupted.

'Yes.'

'Well, if you want my opinion, I think it was probably just a prank. You know, some of those students have nothing better to do . . . ' He reached over and began rummaging through the papers on his desk. 'Here's the invoice. I replaced the wire and added the towing charge . . . Oh, and you wanted us to put on the new snow tires, right?'

'Yes . . . that's fine. Thank you,' Paris

mumbled as she opened her purse. 'Is a check all right?'

'No problem, miss,' came the reply.

Paris paid the bill and then transferred her books and briefcase to her car, but as she drove home through the darkened streets, her head was spinning.

It wasn't simply a prank — she was sure of it. Someone had deliberately sabotaged her car, and the very notion brought a surge of anger to the surface. Why would anyone do such a thing?

It had to have been done sometime on Friday, she reasoned. The car sat in the same parking spot every day, making it an easy target for anyone.

She cast her thoughts back to Friday evening, remembering how surprised she'd been when the car hadn't started. She remembered, too, that Neil Pavan had been in the parking lot. And she'd had the distinct impression he'd been waiting for her.

Could Neil have been the one who cut the wire? He'd seemed nervous at the time, and when they'd heard Adam approach, Neil had made a hasty retreat.

But why would Neil, or anyone for that matter, want to sabotage her car? A shiver of apprehension chased along her nerve endings. Could this incident somehow be connected to the basketball players? She'd told them she'd have to take some action — and in accordance with the rules governing the college, suspension from the basketball team was the next step. But what had they hoped to gain?

With this question still circling in her head, she pulled into the grocery store on the edge of town. She bought a barbecued chicken and a small container of macaroni salad, and as she drove the rest of the way home, she found she was still unable to come to grips with the fact that someone had deliberately tampered with her car.

Though she wanted to believe the mechanic's explanation, she couldn't help wondering why the students had waited this long to play the prank.

Paris shook her head. She was being foolish and much too melodramatic, she told herself as she closed the car door and hurried inside.

After switching on the lights, she took off her coat and carried the bag containing her dinner into the kitchen. When she sat down to eat, she found her thoughts returning to the candlelight dinner she'd shared with Adam and she felt a stab of pain at the memory.

He'd seemed a different person that evening. And much as she hated to admit it, she'd been drawn to him in a way she'd found disturbing.

Suddenly, Paris understood how powerless Francesca must have felt twelve years ago. Francesca had been a young girl of eighteen then, vulnerable and susceptible to the charm and charisma that were an integral element of Adam Kincaid.

But it was all a façade, Paris reminded herself, as her thoughts switched once more to the scene in Stuart Unger's office when Adam, with his own words, confirmed everything Unger had said about him.

And what would happen, she wondered, if she had to recommend that the players be suspended? Would Adam agree?

Suddenly the telephone in the hall rang, effectively breaking into her thoughts, and with a sigh she rose to answer it.

'Hello!' she said softly. 'Hello?' she repeated a moment later. Her greeting was met with total and complete silence. 'Is anyone there?' she asked, as some inner sense told her there was indeed someone on the other end of the line. But who? 'Hello!'

Paris gently replaced the receiver, telling herself it had been a wrong number, nothing more. But as she returned to the kitchen and began to clean up, she found she couldn't easily dismiss the feeling of unease that washed over her.

6

Paris paid for her ticket and smiled at several students she recognized as she made her way to the gymnasium. The noise spilling through the open doors was deafening. The game had already begun.

She squeezed her way into the gym and climbed the first set of bleachers, hoping to find an empty seat. Judging by the shouts of encouragement and applause going on around her, it wasn't difficult to realize that the team was indeed a favorite with the local community as well as with the students.

Halfway up the first set of bleachers, she found a couple of empty seats on the end of a row.

Paris was soon totally immersed in the game, jumping out of her seat with the crowd whenever the Brockton Bears scored a point. As the game progressed, the speed and agility of the players from both teams impressed her, and the excitement and atmosphere in the gymnasium was electric.

When the buzzer for halftime sounded, Paris sank back in her seat in relief. Her heart was pounding, and the fact that the score was a tie was an indication of just how closely matched the two teams were.

Throughout the first half of the game, she'd paid particular attention to the six students with whom she was having trouble. Stuart Unger had told her they were all valuable players, and she recognized now that if she had to carry through her threat to suspend one or more of them, the team would certainly suffer.

Some of her fellow supporters joined the rush to buy refreshments, but Paris remained in her seat. Her mind was occupied with the burning question of exactly what she would do if any of the players failed to hand in the assignment, or failed the assignment itself.

'I thought I recognized you.' Adam's voice broke into her reverie and she glanced up in surprise to see him standing beside her.

'Hi,' she said, and as she gazed into his honey-gold eyes, she felt her pulse pick up speed. He was dressed in jeans, a rust-colored pullover sweater and a brown leather jacket and Paris thought he looked even more attractive than usual.

'Hi, yourself,' he replied, his mouth turning up into a dazzling smile that did strange things to her heart. 'Mind if I join you?' he asked, but before she could reply, he brushed past her and sat down in the empty seat next to hers. 'Quite an exciting game, isn't it?' he went on, as he slid his arm along the bench behind her and angled his body toward her.

'That's an understatement,' she replied, trying to ignore the fact that his knees were nudging hers. Her fingers curled nervously around the jacket resting on her lap and she stiffened, wishing, not for the first time, she could control her response to this man.

'Wait for the second half,' he said, his tone almost boastful. 'The Bears will blow them away.'

'How can you be so sure?' Paris asked as she sat back in her seat, angling her knees away from his. The action, however, brought about an entirely different result. Behind her, his hands made contact with her neck, sending a jolt of electricity shooting through her, trapping her breath in her throat and causing her heart to skip several beats.

Her eyes flew to his and for a tense moment their gazes held. Paris was the first to move, breaking the spell and the contact, but it was too late. Her heart was spinning like a spaceship in orbit, and a tingling heat lingered in the spot where Adam's hand had rested. She fought to regain her composure, praying silently Adam hadn't noticed her reaction.

Adam watched the play of emotions

flitting across her features and felt the tension radiating from her. The look of alarm he'd seen in her eyes a moment ago surprised him and an emotion he couldn't define stirred to life within him.

The woman intrigued him, he admitted it. He'd caught sight of her when she'd arrived and watched with interest as she found a seat. Since her arrival, his concentration on the game had diminished considerably, and when the whistle for halftime blew, he'd immediately made his way to where she was sitting.

Though he'd always made it a rule never to date a fellow staff member, there was something about Paris Ford that drew him. She seemed familiar somehow, as if perhaps he'd met her before, but for the life of him he couldn't remember where.

The pull of attraction he felt was strong indeed, and judging by her reaction a moment ago, he knew she wasn't indifferent to him. It was a situation he fully intended to explore.

Calmly now, he picked up the conversation. 'The Bears will win,' he said, emphasizing the words. 'They've got the stamina, the strength, and the skill that makes them the best team in this division, and that will eventually take them to the national championships.'

'It isn't over yet,' Paris said, glad that her voice sounded normal. She kept her eyes averted and almost sighed with relief when the players returned from their dressing rooms. Fans, too, were returning to their seats, eager for the game to resume.

'Mind if I stay and watch the second half?' Adam asked.

'Of course not,' Paris said and shrugged her shoulders, hoping to give the impression that she didn't care what he did.

Right from the outset of the second half, the action was fast and furious and Paris was soon caught up in the game, almost managing to forget the man sitting next to her. But when Neil Pavan scored a three-pointer to put the team ahead, Paris let out a whoop and turning to Adam, grinned at him in sheer joy.

Adam grinned engagingly back at her, an action that sent her heart reeling, and for the remainder of the game she was all too aware of the man seated beside her.

Throughout the second half, Paris noticed that the students who were controlling the play, who carried the offensive and who scored the highest number of points were the same students who were making her job very difficult — the students failing English . . . the students in line for suspension.

Adam's prediction that the Bears would win, and handily, came true. When the final whistle blew, the Bears had won by a clear margin of twenty points. As the cheering fans applauded enthusiastically, Paris joined in, admitting to herself that as a team, the Brockton Bears were dynamic and quite possibly unbeatable.

Paris slipped on her jacket, and as the noise gradually began to subside, she waited for a break in the crowd. With Adam right behind her, she joined the throng of fans making their way to floor level.

There was considerable jostling from the crowd, and as they reached the floor a group of overzealous students from the opposing team jumped down from the bleachers nearby and made a rush for the door.

Almost before she was aware of what was happening, Paris was spun around and shoved unceremoniously against Adam. She felt his arms go around her and before she could react or protest he crushed her against his tall frame, burying her face protectively in the curve of his neck.

Sensations, the like of which she'd never felt before, were suddenly spiraling through her. The slightly rough texture of his jaw grazed her forehead and as she drew a ragged breath she inhaled a scent that was all male and wildly exciting. His warmth and strength enveloped her like a magical cloak until all she could hear was the thunderous roar of her blood as it raced through her veins.

He held her for what seemed an eternity, but what in fact was no more than ten seconds. But during those seconds, her whole world seemed to shift and change, as if an earthquake had occurred, leaving her with the feeling that nothing would ever be the same again.

'Sorry.' Adam spoke the word into her ear before he eased her away from him. 'Fists were flying there for a minute, and you were right in the line of fire,' he explained. 'I didn't squash you, did I?' he asked, concern in his voice and in his eyes.

'A little,' Paris replied, hoping that would partially explain her state of breathlessness.

'Come on, let's get out of here,' he said, and with his arm around her, he guided her through the crowd and out into the chilly night where some exuberant fans were being quietly dispersed by several security guards.

'Where's your car?' Adam asked.

'Over by the administration building,' she told him.

'Mine, too,' he said, steering her past a couple of students who were still celebrating.

Paris said nothing as they made their way to the parking lot, too distracted by the fact that Adam's arm was still around her. She found she liked the weight on her shoulder, and the feeling of being protected that went with it. There were too many things about Adam Kincaid that she liked.

Though the parking lot was relatively well lit, Paris was glad of the shadows which helped to hide the disappointment she felt when they reached her car and Adam withdrew his arm.

'Thanks for the escort,' she said, extracting her keys from her jacket pocket.

'No problem,' he assured her.

Paris turned to her car, but the simple task of unlocking the door seemed somehow impossible as her fingers fumbled with the key.

'Shall I . . . ?' Adam asked, his voice directly behind her.

'Thanks, I've got it,' she said with relief as the key slid into place and the lock popped open. She turned to face him. 'Thanks again for your help,' she said, lifting her eyes to meet his.

'My pleasure,' he said.

Paris licked lips that were dry, and for the second time that evening, she was aware of a tension crackling between them that was impossible to ignore. She dropped her gaze but only fractionally, and she found herself staring at his mouth. To her astonishment she was suddenly assailed with a longing to feel his lips on hers and to know the mastery of his kiss.

Paris felt her face grow warm and to hide the telltale blush sweeping over her, she turned abruptly away and

131

opened her car door. Not until she was seated and belted in did she dare to look at Adam. He was leaning on the open door smiling at her, and Paris was almost sure he'd known exactly what she'd been thinking a few moments ago.

Adam watched the blush on her face deepen before she hurriedly looked away from him and turned the key to start the car's motor.

'Drive carefully,' he said as he moved to close her door.

'Goodnight,' Paris replied.

As he closed the door, Adam sensed her relief at being able to escape and as the Volkswagen pulled away, he smiled after her. He'd seen the look of anticipation on her face a few moments ago, and he'd been more than tempted to answer each and every question he'd seen reflected in the depths of those luminous green eyes.

He shook his head as he crossed now to his own car. Fool! Why hadn't he kissed her? He'd wanted to, perhaps more than he was willing to admit. The urge to discover once and for all if the air of innocence about her was real or simply a ruse to entice a man had been strong, and strangely now he felt a sharp sense of loss. How could he have let such a golden opportunity slip away?

As he drove from the parking lot he vowed that next time, he wouldn't let her escape quite so easily.

*　*　*

On Thursday evening Paris stood staring at the clothes hanging in her closet, telling herself the reason for her indecision as to what to wear to the wine-and-cheese party had nothing whatsoever to do with the fact that Adam would be there.

Since the basketball game, she'd tried to banish all thoughts of him from her mind, but to her dismay, the more she told herself not to think about Adam, the more often he seemed to pop into her head.

During the past few days the weather had turned wet and windy, and the snow had disappeared almost as though it had never been.

As the day of the deadline for the assignments drew near, a new kind of tension began to build inside her. Only one more day and the suspense would be over, she told her reflection, as she pulled on the calf-length, multicolored skirt and red mohair sweater that was one of her favorite outfits.

When the telephone rang, she jumped involuntarily and dropped the hanger onto the hardwood floor.

'Stop it!' she chided herself, but her heart was already beginning to pound. She stared at the phone. Not again!

The first call had come on Monday night, before the basketball game. Since then, she'd lost count of how many calls she'd had. Sometimes they awakened her in the middle of the night, but there was never anyone there. That was the frustrating and frightening part of it.

The first call had annoyed her more

than frightened her, but with each subsequent call, her reluctance to answer the phone had steadily increased.

No one ever spoke. The silence was a threat in itself. She'd even thought of going out and buying an answering machine, thinking that might deter the caller, but she'd abandoned the idea, refusing to let herself be intimidated.

When the phone rang for the fourth time, Paris grabbed for the receiver on her bedside table.

'Hello? Oh, it's you, Lucy. Hi,' Paris said as a feeling of relief washed over her.

'You are going to the party tonight, aren't you?' Lucy asked.

'Yes, I'll be there,' Paris replied.

'I haven't seen you for a couple of days, so I thought I'd give you a quick call and remind you just in case,' Lucy said.

'Thanks, Lucy. See you there. 'Bye,' Paris said before she hung up.

Annoyed with herself for her reaction, Paris bent to retrieve the hanger from the floor. Just as she began to straighten, the phone rang again. Paris smiled as she reached for it this time. What had Lucy forgotten to tell her? She wondered.

'Hello?' The silence that greeted her instantly sent a flutter of alarm chasing through her. She fought back fear, biting down on her lower lip to stop it from trembling.

Anger and frustration came to her rescue. 'I know you're there,' she said angrily. 'I know you can hear me. What do you want?'

The silence on the other end was somehow more threatening than usual tonight, and as quickly as it came, her anger vanished, replaced by a feeling of helplessness. 'Why are you doing this?' she asked in a voice that was unsteady now. Tears filled her eyes. 'Damn you!' she said, moments before she slammed down the receiver. 'I will not cry,' she said, fighting now to keep the tears from overflowing.

By the time Paris arrived at the

caféteria in the north building, she was once more in control. The wine-and-cheese party was well under way, and as she glanced around at the faces of the people she worked with, she wished there was someone she could confide in.

She picked up a glass of white wine from the table and began to fill a paper plate from the variety of cheeses displayed.

'Paris, there you are.' Raymond Chancellor joined her, his smile wide, his greeting friendly.

'Raymond. Hi! How are you?' she replied.

'There's an empty table right over there. Go sit down. I'll replenish my plate and join you,' he added, indicating the table nearby.

Paris did as he suggested, and as she waited for Raymond she scanned the room, acknowledging the greetings she received from a number of the teachers she knew.

When her glance came to rest on

Adam she felt her heart kick wildly against her rib cage in urgent response. He was dressed in a charcoal business suit, a gray vest, a white shirt and a patterned tie that had to be pure silk.

She had never seen him look more devastating, and it was all she could do to drag her eyes away from him when Raymond took the seat next to hers.

'So bring me up-to-date,' Raymond said. 'What have you been doing since you came back from your holiday?'

Throughout her conversation with Raymond, Paris found her glance continually straying to Adam, watching him as he wandered around the room, stopping to talk to everyone he met.

He appeared to be totally relaxed and in command, and Paris couldn't help noticing how he seemed to put everyone at ease. He had a style and charm that set him apart from any other man she'd ever known, and as she continued to watch him, she found herself wishing he would bestow one of his smiles on her.

'If you'll excuse me, Paris,' she heard Raymond say, 'I see John Clements over there. His daughter left for Europe right after Christmas. I want to ask if he's heard from her.'

'Fine,' Paris said. 'See you later.'

For the next half hour, Paris made her way around the room, stopping to chat here and there, conscious all the while of Adam's exact location.

It was while she stood with Lucy, discussing the dismal weather conditions, that she saw Adam come to a halt in front of Stuart Unger. Though she couldn't hear the conversation that ensued, it was punctuated with smiles and what appeared to Paris to be good-hearted backslapping.

Beside her, Lucy was talking about Josh, her latest boyfriend, but Paris found it increasingly difficult to concentrate on her friend's chatter. Her eyes were drawn like a magnet to the two men across the room.

When Stuart Unger glanced toward her, Paris quickly looked away, nodding and smiling at Lucy, who was too caught up in what she was saying to notice Paris's preoccupation. After a few moments, Paris ventured to look in Adam's direction once more, only to find herself the focus of his attention.

He was staring at her intently as he listened to whatever Stuart Unger was saying, and she had the distinct impression she was the subject under discussion.

She managed to keep her smile in place as she nodded in acknowledgment of Adam's friendly wave, but as she turned back to Lucy, a feeling of depression slowly began to settle over her.

When at last Lucy came to the end of her dissertation, Paris bit back a sigh. 'I'd love a cup of coffee. How about you?' she asked her friend.

'Not for me, thanks,' Lucy replied. 'I think I'll go and powder my nose. Catch up with you later,' she added, before scurrying away.

Paris wound her way to the table that

held the coffee urn and quickly poured herself a cup of the steaming liquid. For her, the evening had suddenly gone flat, and she decided that as soon as she finished her coffee she'd leave.

'So, this is where you're hiding,' Adam said, and at the teasing quality of his voice, Paris felt her pulse accelerate at an alarming rate.

'I wasn't hiding,' Paris replied, turning to face him. She kept her expression guarded, but there was nothing she could do to control her erratic heartbeat.

She brought a cup to her lips, and sipping the hot, bitter liquid, studied him surreptitiously through lowered lashes. It was quite unfair, she thought dejectedly, that one man should be so attractive.

'How's your uncle?' she asked.

'He's much better, thanks,' Adam replied and Paris heard the relief hidden beneath his words, and saw, too, the flash of emotion in the depths of his gold-speckled eyes. 'He's beginning to argue with the doctors and nurses, so he must be improving.'

'That's great,' she said. 'And Lillian?'

'She's just pleased to hear George kicking up a fuss, again. If he's complaining, she knows he's feeling better.'

'I must call her,' Paris said, remembering her promise.

'She'd like that,' Adam responded. 'Oh, by the way. I've been meaning to ask you — did you solve that little problem you came to see me about . . . those students you were having trouble with? Did you get it sorted out?'

Paris was hard-pressed to hide the shock she felt at his words. His question confirmed that he and Stuart Unger had indeed been talking about her . . .

Anger surged to life inside her and she was tempted, for a moment, to dump what remained of her coffee all over him. But her good manners prevailed and she set the cup on the table beside her.

'Not quite. But I'm working on it,' she said, a cutting edge to her voice now that was unmistakable.

Adam blinked, caught off guard by the anger in her tone. What on earth had he said? he wondered. But before he could ask, she spoke again.

'If you'll excuse me. I was just leaving.'

Before he could stop her, before he could even react, she turned and strode off.

Adam's first instinct was to go after her and demand to know what had made her so angry. But he'd only taken two steps when he heard a familiar voice call his name. Much as he wanted to ignore its owner, the voice belonged to John Fisher, a member of the board. Cursing under his breath, Adam turned to face the man bearing down on him.

Paris grabbed her raincoat and purse from the coatrack inside the caféteria door. Outside, it had stopped raining, and by the time she reached her car, her temper had cooled considerably.

When she'd seen Adam and Unger talking together, they'd looked as thick as thieves, and a feeling of disappointment had stabbed at her. But as she unlocked the car door, she wondered why her stubborn heart refused to believe that Adam was as insensitive and ruthless a man as Stuart Unger appeared to be.

Paris put the key in the ignition and turned it. This action was met with utter and complete silence. She couldn't believe it! She tried again — one, two, three more times, but to no avail.

Dear heaven! Had her car been tampered with again? Even as she wanted to deny it was true, she knew instinctively that the wire the mechanic had mentioned had been cut again.

It was the last straw in an evening that had been a trial in more ways than one. Dropping her head on the steering wheel, she began to cry.

Seconds later the car door was yanked open and Paris gasped. Through tear-filled eyes she glanced up to see Adam towering over her. Before she could think or speak he pulled her from the car and into his arms.

7

'Paris, what is it? What happened?' Adam asked anxiously as he held the sobbing figure tightly in his arms.

He'd followed her as soon as he'd been able to leave John Fisher, and as he'd hurried toward the parking lot he kept expecting to see her drive away. But when he'd reached the car and had seen her slumped dejectedly over the wheel, a feeling of fear had clutched at his heart.

'Please, don't cry,' he continued softly as he eased her body away from his. 'What is it? What's wrong? Are you hurt?'

She took a ragged breath, slowly shaking her head, and the relief that washed over him was overwhelming. He put his finger under her chin and gently urged her to look at him. 'Hey, it can't be that bad, surely?' He wiped away a tear with his thumb.

'I'm fine. It's nothing, really,' Paris said, unevenly. She was finding Adam's tender concern infinitely disturbing, and as his thumb gently caressed her cheek she felt a shiver of response dance across her nerve endings. Lifting her gaze to meet his, she felt her heart skitter to a halt at the fiery glow she could see in the depths of his golden eyes.

Before she even had time to draw breath, before the notion that he was going to kiss her could even register in her brain, his mouth came down on hers, obliterating everything but the sensations suddenly rocketing through her.

His lips were rough and demanding, and though tentative at first, she soon found herself responding with an urgency that matched his. She'd been kissed before, but never like this . . . no, never like this. Tiny explosions of sensation sent new and unfamiliar messages to every cell, awakening a need she'd never known she could feel.

The pressure from his mouth grew ever more urgent and her lips parted and as his tongue teased and tantalized, a new and more compelling need began to build inside her.

Sweetness, softness, innocence — they were all there and much more, Adam thought as he feverishly explored lips that were responding in a way that was driving him to distraction. When her mouth opened beneath his, he almost moaned aloud at the wonder of it, as he delved deeper into the dark recess that held secrets he had to know.

Need spiraled through him, and desire quickly followed, and suddenly Adam was fighting to contain emotions far stronger and more powerful than he'd ever felt before.

She was out of control, totally and completely at the mercy of this man who had taught her in one swift and easy lesson the precise meaning of desire. And with each second that passed, he pulled her closer and closer to the center of the fire, taking her deeper and deeper into the white-hot vortex . . .

Was this how Francesca had felt? The question dropped into her mind like a meteor falling out of the sky, shattering the moment and sending her plummeting to earth with lightning speed.

With a cry that came straight from her heart, Paris wrenched herself free of Adam's embrace. 'Is this how you seduced Francesca?' she asked shakily, a mixture of pain and anger threading her voice.

'Francesca?' Adam's breathing was ragged as he repeated the name.

'Yes . . . Francesca,' Paris continued. 'Surely you haven't forgotten her?' she said, bitterness edging her tone now.

'What does she have to do with this?' Adam asked, in a tightly controlled voice.

'She was my cousin . . . She loved you. But you tossed her aside and ruined her life . . . or have you forgotten that, too?' Paris watched the blood drain from Adam's face. That he was shocked by her words was painfully obvious, and for a fleeting moment she felt a twinge of regret.

'You're Francesca's cousin?' His voice was little more than a whisper.

'Yes. And I was there, at my aunt's house,' Paris hurried on. 'I saw how devastated Francesca was the day you turned your back on her and walked out of her life.'

Adam ran a hand through his hair. 'I see,' he said, staring at her intently now. 'I thought there was something vaguely familiar about you. You were at the top of the stairs.'

'You saw me?' Paris was unable to hide her surprise.

'I saw a child,' he said bitingly.

'I'm not a child any longer,' she replied, a note of defiance in her voice.

Adam's eyes traveled the length of her, and she felt her skin prickle in instant response. 'Isn't that what we both discovered just now?' Adam asked calmly, and at the implication of his words, a feeling of anger burst to life within her.

'You're despicable,' she almost shouted at him.

'And you're a fool,' he replied with barely suppressed anger. 'What happened between you and me a few moments ago had nothing to do with Francesca. You'd do well to remember that.' He turned to leave, then changed his mind. 'Oh, there is one more thing before I go,' he added in a voice that was as icy as an arctic glacier. 'If you want to play judge and jury, I'd advise you to make sure you have all the facts.' With that, Adam strode off, leaving Paris staring in stunned silence after him.

Paris wasn't sure how long she stood there. Her thoughts were in chaos, her mind grappling with the implication of Adam's parting words.

His anger had been very real. Could it be she was missing some of the facts? Suddenly Paris recalled the comments Lillian had made on the night of the snow-storm. Had Francesca lied?

'Hey, Paris. Are you all right?' A voice broke the silence, bringing her wayward thoughts back to the present.

Glad of the shadows that helped to hide her tear-stained face, Paris turned to see Lucy walking toward her. 'Hi . . . Yes, I'm all right,' Paris replied, keeping her eyes averted.

'Are you sure?' Lucy asked as she drew closer.

'Well . . . actually it's my car,' Paris said, suddenly remembering her predicament. 'It won't start. I was trying to decide whether to call Gibson's Garage or just call a taxi,' she explained.

'The garage will be closed by now,' Lucy said. 'I'll give you a ride home if you like.'

'That would be great, Lucy. Thanks.' Paris reached into her car and removed the keys and her purse.

'Do you want me to pick you up in the morning?' Lucy asked when she pulled into Paris's driveway half an hour later.

'I'd appreciate that. Thanks,' Paris replied.

Lucy waited until Paris was safely inside before she blinked her car's headlights and drove away. Locking the door behind her, Paris slipped off her coat and made her way to her bedroom.

She undressed slowly, then removed her makeup, noticing that her face still held a trace of tears. She climbed into bed, but sleep was the furthest thing from her mind. Instead, she replayed in her head the events of the evening, an evening that had culminated in a kiss she wouldn't soon forget.

All she'd been aware of was Adam and the sensations he'd so swiftly aroused in her, catapulting her into a world that was all sensation, a world she'd only dreamed about.

The depth of her response had shaken her to the core. But at the back of her mind, there lingered the memory that this was the same man who'd callously shattered her cousin's hopes and dreams.

She realized now that she'd thrown Francesca's name at Adam as a means of self-preservation, needing to remind herself of the kind of man he was and what he was capable of. She'd acted in self-defense, instinctively protecting herself against forces she'd had no control over . . . because during those incredible moments when he kissed her, she'd realized for the first time in her life that she was in danger . . . in grave danger, of losing her heart.

Tears suddenly filled her eyes and she let them slip from beneath her lashes to trickle onto the pillow beneath her head.

He'd said she was a fool, and she supposed she was, but not for the reason he'd stated. He'd accused her of playing judge and jury, said that she didn't know all the facts . . . but she'd been there, she'd seen with her own eyes . . . heard with her own ears.

Paris brought her thoughts to a halt. She'd watched the drama unfold, but she hadn't been a central character.

Most of what she'd learned, she'd learned by eavesdropping. Had she misinterpreted what happened? It was a question she'd never asked herself before.

But even if she had misinterpreted part of what she'd heard, Francesca's pregnancy had been real. The letter Aunt Margaret sent months later had confirmed that. Francesca had lost the baby, and as a result of the emotional turmoil she and her mother had had to sell everything and leave Brockton.

There had been no mention of Adam in the letter, but he'd been the only one who'd come to the house, who'd talked to Francesca, and judging by what Paris had heard of that conversation, he had to have been the man Francesca had been involved with.

Perhaps she herself had only been a child, as Adam had so scathingly pointed out, but that didn't mean she hadn't understood what was going on.

He was wrong. She had known the facts — not all of them, she would give him that, but certainly enough to convince her she hadn't been mistaken.

Paris gazed up at the ceiling as the turmoil raging inside her began to ease. But as she lay in the darkness, she silently acknowledged that there was one thing Adam had been right about. The kiss they'd shared had had nothing whatsoever to do with Francesca, and everything to do with the overwhelming attraction she felt for him.

But she had quite enough to contend with right now, what with anonymous telephone calls, the tampering with her car and the problem of the basketball students — her feelings for Adam were a complication she could well do without.

★　★　★

The next morning, Lucy was as good as her word, picking Paris up and driving her to the college. Before leaving for work, Paris had called the garage to arrange for a mechanic to drive out and take a look at her car. He'd assured her he'd try to fix it on the spot, and failing that, would tow it to the garage once more.

Paris was glad that she had a busy schedule that morning, which helped to keep thoughts of Adam at bay. She still felt a little bruised by their encounter the previous evening, and she wasn't sure she was ready to face him just yet.

At lunchtime she returned to her office. The mechanic called to let her know that he'd already driven out to the college and fixed her car. He confirmed that it had indeed been tampered with once again, and though the news came as no surprise to Paris, she was at a loss to know what to do. She could only assume that the culprits had to be the basketball students, and assume, too, that they were responsible for the anonymous phone calls, which were meant to frighten her.

They were obviously trying to scare her into abandoning her efforts to enforce the college rules. But she in turn was determined to ignore their tactics and stay true to her principles and those of the college.

As the deadline she'd set for the basketball students approached, her apprehension grew. It was becoming increasingly difficult to feel optimistic that things would work out.

In an attempt to take her mind off the problem, Paris put a call through to Lillian Boone.

'Hello,' Lillian said.

'Lillian, it's Paris Ford.'

'Paris! How lovely to hear from you.' Lillian's voice was warm and sincere.

'I called to ask how George is doing, and you, too, of course.'

'George is much better,' Lillian replied. 'In fact, the doctor told me they hope to be able to release him from hospital early next week.'

'But that's wonderful,' Paris said, pleased to hear the news.

'I can't tell you how good it will be to have him home,' Lillian said.

'And what about you? You're not

overdoing things, are you?'

'I'm fine,' Lillian replied. 'But I don't know what I would have done if Adam hadn't been here. Even with his busy schedule, he still finds time to pop in and see George. He wasn't able to last night, of course, because of the wine-and-cheese party. How was it?'

'Very nice,' Paris replied cautiously, managing to instil a little enthusiasm into her voice. Lillian's mention of Adam had effectively brought her thoughts back to the events in the parking lot. Resolutely, she pushed them aside. 'Well, I'm really pleased about George,' Paris said, preparing to end the conversation.

'Listen, my dear,' Lillian quickly cut in. 'Are you busy on Sunday?'

'I . . . Well, no. Why?' Paris stammered.

'Would you join me for dinner?' Lillian asked, and before Paris could reply she hurried on. 'Adam is going out of town, and I'd appreciate the company.'

Paris hesitated, but she couldn't bring herself to refuse. 'Then I'd love to,' she said.

'Good,' Lillian replied. 'Come at five and we'll have a sherry before dinner. See you then.'

Paris replaced the receiver and stared at it for several minutes. She should have declined the invitation, but she hadn't had the heart to refuse, and when she'd heard that Adam would not be in attendance, the decision had been that much easier.

He was a threat to her peace of mind, and though she knew she couldn't avoid him altogether, she hoped to be able to keep contact with him at a minimum.

A knock at the door of her office startled her. 'Come in!' she called.

The door opened to reveal Neil Pavan holding several sheets of paper in his hand. 'Hello, Neil,' she said in a friendly tone.

'Here's that assignment, Miss Ford,' Neil said as he approached her desk and held out the papers.

'Thanks,' Paris said, taking them from him. 'I was at the game Monday night. You were great.'

At her compliment, Neil's face turned a light shade of pink. 'Thanks,' he mumbled. 'I gotta go,' he added, and turned to leave.

'Are you going home for the weekend?' Paris asked, knowing that Neil came from a small town on the Oregon/Washington border.

'I wish,' Neil replied. 'No, we've got a big game tomorrow night against the Rogues. The bus leaves in an hour . . . '

'You mean the Bears have an away game this weekend?' Paris asked.

'Yes,' Neil said. 'At Richmond College. It's up near Seattle. The Rogues won the divisional championship last year and right now, the way things stand in the league, the Rogues have the same win record as we do. All we have to do is beat them tomorrow night and again next Saturday when they come here to play us,' he explained.

'I see — I think,' Paris said shaking her head in confusion.

Neil smiled. 'Well, I have to run. See you in class on Monday,' he said as he closed the door.

By three o'clock only the two students from Neil's class had come by to hand in their work. Not one of the three senior students appeared.

She'd gone out of her way to give the students a chance and though she wasn't altogether surprised, she was disappointed. The time for compromises was over. She had no choice now but to go to Adam and explain the problem, and ask that he suspend Jason French, Rick Diamond and Barry Kralic from the basketball team.

But there seemed little point in trying to enforce the matter today. Even if she could locate Adam, there didn't seem to be much point in suspending the players, especially if they were already on the bus on their way to the game at Richmond College.

She would make an appointment to

see Adam first thing Monday morning, but she was adamant in her own mind that should he refuse to take action, she would not hesitate to take the matter to the board of directors.

By Sunday afternoon, Paris was growing restless. She'd spent the best part of the weekend reading through and marking numerous papers, including the assignments handed in by Neil and the other two students. She was pleased that the three freshmen had improved their mark significantly.

She showered and dressed in a navy wool skirt and matching top, realizing that she was looking forward to her dinner engagement with Lillian Boone.

The snow had all but disappeared and the rain, too, had stopped. Outside it was cold and dry and the sky was free of clouds as Paris drove through town. Dusk was descending as she pulled into the winding drive-way leading to the Boone house.

The doorbell's summons was answered by a young woman in a maid's uniform.

After taking off her coat, Paris followed her to the spacious living room that overlooked the beautiful gardens at the front of the house.

'Hello, Paris. How lovely to see you,' Lillian said, holding out her hands and smiling a welcome. She gave Paris's hands a squeeze. 'Your hands are cold. Come and warm them,' she said, indicating the fire burning in the fireplace.

'Thank you for inviting me,' Paris said politely, pleased to see that Lillian was indeed looking less anxious and more rested than the last time Paris had seen her.

'May I pour you a sherry?' Lillian asked.

'A small one, thank you,' Paris replied.

Lillian crossed to the liquor cabinet. 'It's so nice to have female company for a change,' Lillian said as she half filled two small sherry glasses. Returning to where Paris sat in the armchair by the fire, Lillian handed her a glass. 'Now then,' Lillian continued as she sat down on the love seat nearby. 'Tell me how you're doing. Are you still enjoying your work? No doubt the students keep you on your toes,' she remarked.

'I love my job,' Paris said, her tone sincere. 'And yes, the students are quite a challenge,' she added.

Conversation continued on a general vein until the young woman who'd answered the door earlier appeared to inform them that dinner was ready.

Lillian linked her arm in Paris's as they made their way toward the oak-paneled doors that lead into the adjoining dining room.

Dinner was delicious and consisted of thinly sliced roast beef with Yorkshire pudding, roast potatoes and creamed carrots. Paris couldn't recall enjoying a meal more.

Lillian talked a good deal about George and what the doctors had told her to expect regarding his continued recovery. Paris listened, asking the occasional question.

'Adam has dropped in almost every day at the hospital to see George,' Lillian said, appreciation and love for Adam evident in her tone. 'I don't know how he's found the time,' she added.

At the mention of Adam, Paris felt her pulse pick up speed. She was surprised to discover that she wanted Lillian to linger on the topic of her nephew, then perhaps she might learn more about the man who affected her as no other had. But before Paris could ask or say anything Lillian spoke again.

'But then Adam has always been that kind of man — eager to lend a helping hand no matter who or what the problem might be.' Lillian was silent for a long moment. 'That's how he became embroiled in that business with that girl all those years ago,' she went on, ' . . . and look what happened. But enough about that,' she hurried on, her face creasing in a frown now, as though she regretted having spoken. 'Let's have our coffee by the fire, shall we?' she suggested, rising from the table.

'That sounds lovely,' Paris said with a smile, but as she made her way to the living room, her mind was filled with questions. Had Lillian been referring to Francesca? It seemed the logical conclusion. But surely Lillian's comment that Adam had only been trying to help wasn't right.

When they returned to the living room, Paris resumed her seat by the fire, but before she could ask Lillian for a more detailed explanation, the maid arrived carrying a tray with a beautiful silver coffee service.

Just as Lillian finished pouring coffee into two cups the door to the living room opened and Paris glanced up in surprise to see Adam entering the room.

'Adam, you're back early,' Lillian said and smiled warmly at her nephew. 'We were just talking about you.'

'Really?' Adam said and Paris felt his glance dart in her direction. She deliberately avoided his gaze, concentrating instead on accepting the coffee cup Lillian held out to her.

'Thank you,' she mumbled, but all the while her heart was drumming a frantic tattoo against her breast, reacting the way it always did whenever Adam was near.

'Have I missed dinner?' he asked, coming farther into the room.

'We only just finished,' Lillian told him. 'Would you like me to ask Molly to fix you a plate?'

'That would be great, thank you,' Adam replied.

'Excuse me a moment, won't you?' Lillian said, turning to Paris.

'Of course,' Paris replied, suddenly wishing she was the one leaving the room. The prospect of being alone with Adam, even for a short time, was playing havoc with her senses.

Adam waited until Lillian closed the door before he crossed to stand with his back to the fireplace. Normally he would have gone to the kitchen himself, but he was curious to know just why

Paris was there.

'What are you doing here?' Adam's tone was cool and only marginally polite.

'Your aunt invited me,' Paris explained, glancing briefly at him, hating the antagonism in his voice, yet knowing the reason for it.

'I'm surprised you accepted,' he continued, 'especially when there was a chance you'd run into me.'

Paris put her cup and saucer back on the tray and stood up. 'I came because I like your aunt, and because she said you would be out of town,' she told him sharply.

Adam smiled, admiring the fact that she had told him the truth. 'And does she know who you are?' he asked softly.

He watched in fascination as she turned angry green eyes to his and not for the first time Adam felt his heart kick against his ribs in reaction to the startling impact of those eyes.

He'd never seen anyone with features quite so perfect. Her blond hair shimmered in the firelight, and her skin had a healthy glow that needed no makeup to enhance its rich coloring.

For the past three days and nights, he hadn't been able to get the image of her, or the memory of the kiss they'd shared, out of his mind. But neither could he forget how the kiss had ended, and the knowledge that she believed him guilty of a crime he hadn't committed had hurt him far more than he'd thought possible.

'If by that you mean that I'm related to Francesca, then no,' Paris replied.

'Then I'd advise you not to tell her,' he went on. At the time, it had come as quite a shock to make the discovery himself, but he felt sure that if Lillian knew, she would feel compelled to set the record straight, if only to assure herself that Paris was aware of the damage Francesca had done with her false accusations.

But Paris had been a child then, Adam reminded himself, and had obviously misunderstood all that had gone on, and though Adam remembered seeing her on the first visit he'd made to the Petrie house, he hadn't seen her on subsequent visits.

In some ways she was still a child, and frustrating though it might be, if a relationship was to develop between them, she had to learn to trust him, but he wanted that trust to come from within.

'There's a plate set out for you in the kitchen,' Lillian said as she rejoined them. 'By the way, I forgot to ask how the basketball game went. Did the Bears win?'

'Yes, but it was quite a nail-biter,' Adam replied with a shake of his head. 'We're one step closer to winning the divisional championship. And if we beat the Rogues again next Saturday when they come here, there'll be no stopping us.'

'Adam went to Seattle with the team,' Lillian explained as she came to sit in the armchair near Paris. 'It's wonderful what those boys have accomplished this year. What a boost it will be to the college if they get to the nationals.'

'And if they lose?' Paris asked, unable to stop herself. She felt Adam's gaze flick to her and as their glances collided, she tried to ignore the shiver of awareness that danced across her skin.

'Then we'll have to deal with it,' Adam said evenly, but there was an alert look in his eyes now as he continued. 'Barring a serious injury to one of the players, I can't honestly see the team losing now.'

'What if one or more players were suspended?' Paris asked, amazed at how calm she felt. She knew this was neither the time nor the place to discuss this issue, but suddenly she wanted to find out just what kind of reaction she could expect from Adam when she dropped what was sure to be a bombshell on Monday.

Adam narrowed his gaze and a look she couldn't decipher came and went in his eyes. The tension between them was almost tangible and suddenly Paris regretted having spoken.

'This discussion is getting much too serious for me,' Lillian said lightly, 'and your dinner must be getting cold, Adam.'

It was the opportunity Paris had been waiting for. 'It's getting late,' she said rising from the chair. 'I think I'll be on my way.'

'So soon?' Lillian asked, disappointment evident in her tone.

'I had a lovely time,' Paris assured her. 'Thank you so much for a delicious dinner.'

'You're very welcome, my dear. I enjoyed our visit,' Lillian said. 'Once George is home, perhaps you'll join us again sometime.'

'I'd love to,' Paris replied leaning forward to kiss Lillian's cheek.

'I'll walk you to your car,' Adam said, drawing a curious look from his aunt.

'There's really no need.' Paris began to cross to the living room door.

'I insist,' Adam answered, and there

was no mistaking the steel edge in his voice that told her clearly his mind was made up.

Paris turned and smiled at Lillian. 'Good night, and give George my best.'

As Paris walked the length of the hall with Adam, she was aware of the rising tension in the man beside her. The maid appeared and quickly located Paris's raincoat, which she handed to Adam, before retreating once more. But as Adam held her coat, and Paris slid her arms into the sleeves, she sensed that the evening was by no means over.

8

'Would you kindly tell me what the hell is going on?' Adam asked the moment they stepped out onto the porch.

Paris turned and stared in silence at Adam. Her first instinct was to deny that she knew what he was talking about, but before she could speak he hurried on.

'And don't tell me you don't know what I mean,' he warned her. 'Whatever it is you were trying to tell me in there, I'd appreciate the whole story . . . now,' he concluded angrily.

Paris glared at him for several moments, aware that her heart was beating frantically against her breast. His gaze never wavered as he waited for her answer.

'I was going to make an appointment to see you on Monday — '

'Forget Monday. Tell me now.' They

were still standing on the porch outside the front door, and as he spoke he took a step toward her.

Paris drew a steadying breath and licked lips that were dry. 'I'm recommending the suspension of three members of the basketball team,' she said.

'You're what?'

Paris swallowed before continuing. 'Jason French, Rick Diamond and Barry Kralic are ineligible to play.'

'You can't be serious!'

'Believe me, I'm very serious,' she replied, annoyance rippling through her. She'd planned to start at the beginning, to explain to him, calmly and unemotionally, how the problem had arisen and the steps she'd already taken in an attempt to solve it.

But on reflection, she'd tried this approach already and he'd sent her packing. This time she had no intention of backing down, not for him or anyone.

'Wait a minute,' Adam said, his

shadowed features looking strangely menacing. 'Are these the same students you came to talk to my uncle about, two weeks ago?'

'That's right,' she replied defiantly.

'But I thought that was only a disciplinary problem. When I asked you about it the other day, you told me you were working on it. Has there been some new development I should know about? I'm not going to suspend those students if all they're guilty of is forgetting to hand in their assignments?'

Paris clenched her teeth, biting back the angry retort threatening to spill forth. She took another deep breath before going on. 'You didn't bother to listen to me then, or let me explain. You simply jumped to conclusions without knowing the facts,' she told him scathingly.

At her words, a bitter smile curled at the corners of Adam's mouth. 'I could accuse you of the same,' he replied harshly.

But Paris ignored the comment. 'There's more to this than a case of undisciplined students,' she retorted angrily. 'The integrity of this college is at stake here, and I doubt very much if your uncle would approve of the way you're handling things,' she added bitingly.

'Let me tell you something,' Adam said with more than a hint of exasperation in his tone now. 'You don't know the half of it. I have no intention of suspending those students because . . .'

'Then I'll go to the board of directors.' Paris cut in. Pushing past him, she hurried down the front stairs, surprised by the pain and disappointment that had washed over her at his words.

She broke into a run, and as she crossed the courtyard to her car, she mumbled under her breath at the stupidity of men in general and Adam in particular. But just as she reached her car a hand gripped her arm, spinning her around.

'You didn't let me finish,' he said with barely concealed rage.

'There's nothing left to say,' she replied, her anger matching his own.

For a long, tension-filled moment, Adam simply stared at her. 'You're absolutely right,' he said, before he hauled her against him and captured her mouth with his.

Though the breath was knocked out of her, Paris instinctively began to struggle. But her efforts were quickly rendered futile and she suddenly found herself responding to the urgent demand of his lips.

Of their own volition, her arms went around his neck urging him closer, and when she felt his hands slide beneath her coat to press her body tightly against his, a shudder of need swept through her, making her gasp.

She'd never known a kiss could drive her to the edge of sanity quite so quickly, nor had she known that a kiss could unleash such an avalanche of passion, hurtling her into a maelstrom of sensation she wasn't sure she would survive.

Her fingers explored the silky texture of his hair, enjoying the feel of it against her skin. But it wasn't enough; she wanted more — needed more, and she wondered at the depth of the emotion steadily gathering strength within her.

Adam gave himself up to the pure joy he felt simply holding Paris in his arms. He could taste her need smoldering just below the surface, and he could feel the urgency growing ever stronger within her.

He'd known desire before, and had accepted the part it played in every man's life, but always on his own terms. Now for the first time in his life, the control he'd prided himself in having was slipping away like snow down a mountainside.

What was there about this woman that had drawn her to him from the start? Normally, he was cautious and careful when it came to relationships, but Paris seemed to have broken through all the barriers to reach inside him and strip away all his defenses.

Her innocence, her sweetness — that's what set her apart from every other woman he'd known, he thought as the kiss drove them ever higher. And while the throbbing ache gnawing at his insides told him he wanted her, he knew that path would only lead to disaster, and she would end up despising him for taking advantage of her, just as she believed he'd taken advantage of Francesca.

At this thought, an intense pain tore through him, causing him to break free of the kiss. Gazing down at her, he watched as her eyes opened to reveal the flames of passion still flickering in their green depths. And suddenly Adam was faced with the realization that what he felt for Paris was much more than simple physical desire.

Somehow, somewhere, she had touched his soul, unlocking his deepest emotions . . .

'Well, well . . . ' he said softly, fighting

to douse the fires still raging within him. 'It would appear we do have something we agree on, after all.'

His remark had the exact effect he'd hoped for, and when her hand made stinging contact with his cheek, he welcomed the pain, which helped to distract him from emotions he wasn't sure he was ready to face.

Paris couldn't believe she'd actually slapped Adam; she'd never hit anyone in her life before. Her action had been purely reflex, arising from the need to hurt the person who'd hurt her, but instead she felt tears of remorse sting her eyes and she had to bite down on the inner softness of her mouth to stop the tears from overflowing.

Turning away, she pulled open her car door and climbed inside. With trembling fingers, she located her keys and as the engine roared to life, she was relieved that Adam didn't make any attempt to stop her.

She reached the end of the driveway and turned onto the street, but she hadn't gone very far before she had to pull off to the side of the road. Fumbling in her purse, she found the small package of tissues she kept there, and it was several moments before she could drive on.

Throughout the journey home, she berated herself for allowing the kiss to happen, and tried, without success, not to think about the wanton way she'd responded to the man she was supposed to despise.

What was there about Adam Kincaid that seemed to call out to her heart and soul?

But before she could ponder on this question further Paris noticed that her house was in total darkness. Perhaps the light bulb by the door had burned out, she thought as she closed her car door and walked toward the house.

As she drew nearer, she sensed something was wrong and a prickle of fear chased down her spine. The front door stood wide-open and at the sight of it, Paris stopped in her tracks. 'Oh, no!' she whispered as her heart began to hammer against her rib cage.

She stood for a moment, undecided whether to enter the house, or turn around and drive to the nearest telephone booth and call the police.

Finally, anger and outrage propelled her forward and she entered the house. She flicked the light switch, instantly illuminating the hall. The eerie silence that met her quickly erased her initial bravado and cautiously now, she made her way toward the kitchen.

Heart still pounding, she stopped in the doorway and holding her breath she pushed open the door and reached for the light switch. The kitchen was empty . . . and her sigh of relief was audible.

Paris glanced toward the stairs leading to the upper floor. Poised and ready to run should the need arise, she listened for the slightest sound, but all she could hear was the frantic beating of her heart.

Just as she entered the living room, the telephone rang, shattering the silence. Paris jumped and fell back against the door, quickly clamping her hand over her mouth to stop the scream rising in her throat. For several seconds she stood unable to move, but as the ringing persisted, she moved toward the alcove where the phone was located.

Who could it be? she wondered as she stared at the instrument. Her anonymous caller? The insistent ringing continued playing havoc with her nerves. On the seventh ring she grabbed the receiver. 'Why are you doing this to me? Leave me alone!' she shouted into the phone, hating the feeling of helplessness engulfing her.

'Paris! What is it? What's wrong?' Adam's anxious voice startled her.

'Adam?' she asked tentatively, wondering if she was dreaming.

'What's going on? Are you all right?' he asked urgently.

'I think someone broke into my house,' Paris answered shakily, feeling the reaction beginning to settle over her.

'I'll be right there,' Adam said, and before she could reply, he hung up.

Paris stood holding the telephone receiver for several seconds. Somehow, the fact that Adam was on his way helped to restore her confidence. Surely if the intruder was still in the house, she would have heard something by now, she reasoned.

Feeling a little braver, she slowly began to make a tour of the house, switching on lights as she passed from room to room. As far as she could tell, nothing appeared to be missing and no damage had been done. She was beginning to wonder if she'd simply forgotten to lock up when she left earlier, but when she opened her bedroom door she caught a faint scent in the air — not perfume — leaving her with a strong impression that someone had been there.

She couldn't stop the shiver of fear that passed through her, but as she glanced around looking for some physical evidence that would confirm her suspicions, everything seemed to be in order . . . Except that she was sure she'd closed the drawers on her dresser. Now they were all open.

Her uneasiness returned and she retreated downstairs to wait for Adam. She'd closed the front door before venturing upstairs, but the chill suddenly sweeping through her now had nothing to do with the cold January temperature outside and everything to do with the growing belief that someone had invaded her privacy.

She returned to the living room, and crossing to the fireplace, she busied herself building a fire. Once the fire was lit, she kept watch at the window, anxious now for Adam to arrive.

When the headlights of a car swept past the window, she hurried from the room to open the front door. At the sight of Adam striding toward her, it was all she could do not to run to him.

'Did you call the police? Are you all right?' he asked, the moment he reached her.

'I'm fine,' Paris replied and silently added *now that you're here*. As she glanced up at him, she was surprised to note how pale and tense he looked. 'And no, I haven't called the police . . . '

'Why not?' Adam demanded as he closed the door behind him and turned anxious eyes to her.

'Because there doesn't appear to be anything missing,' she replied. 'And I'm beginning to wonder if I just forgot to lock up when I left to go to your aunt's earlier,' she told him. Now that he was there with her, all her fears seemed to have vanished.

'Do you always lock the door when you leave?' Adam asked.

'Yes, but . . . '

'Then someone was here,' he quickly cut in. 'I'll check the house.'

'I already did,' she told him, strangely warmed by the fact that he'd believed her when she said she had locked the door.

'Doesn't hurt to double-check,' Adam replied.

'I'll make a pot of coffee,' she said as he strode off down the hall.

Glad to have something to occupy her thoughts, Paris entered the kitchen and crossed to the sink. As she filled the coffee maker with water and measured the grounds, she could hear Adam upstairs, and the noise was somehow comforting.

The soft gurgling of the coffee machine soon filled the kitchen, bringing with it a rich aroma. Paris retrieved two mugs from the cupboard and crossed to the table.

As her glance fell on the table, she noticed a single sheet of paper. She scanned the big bold letters printed on the sheet and as their message registered, a feeling of nausea engulfed her, causing the coffee mugs to slip from her fingers and crash to the floor.

Seconds later Adam burst through the door to see Paris, her face deathly pale, staring at the table. He was at her side in an instant and as his arm went around her, he followed her gaze.

MIND YOUR OWN BUSINESS, TEACHER! OR ELSE!!!

The words screamed at him from the paper, and turning her to face him, he drew her against his chest, fighting down the rage suddenly welling up inside him. Whoever had done this would pay, he vowed silently, as his arms tightened protectively around Paris.

'Hey! Hey. Take it easy. It's all right, I'm right here.' Adam's voice was as soothing as a caress and at his words, the fear clutching at her heart gradually began to subside.

She'd never felt so safe, or so cared for, and as the earthy, masculine scent of him filled her nostrils, it was all she could do not to snuggle closer and kiss the warm column of his throat. It would be heaven to stay here forever, she thought, in something of a daze.

Good Lord! Just what was she thinking about? Annoyed with the direction her thoughts had taken, she pulled away from him. 'I'm sorry. I don't usually fall apart like this,' she mumbled, feeling her face grow warm under his gaze.

'You didn't fall apart,' he chided her gently. 'I'd say your reaction was normal in the circumstances,' he added, and followed his words with a smile.

Paris felt her heart skip a beat in response to the smile. She didn't want to like him . . . didn't want to trust him, but with each encounter she was finding it increasingly difficult to keep him at arm's length. 'Look at the mess . . . ' she said motioning to the pieces of broken stoneware scattered on the floor.

'I'll take care of it,' Adam said. 'Where do you keep your broom?'

'I can do it,' Paris replied as she turned to the cupboard next to the refrigerator.

'Sit!' Adam said and urged her into one of the kitchen chairs. He opened the cupboard and extracted a broom and dustpan, and she watched as he deftly restored the floor to order.

'The coffee . . . ' Paris said and started to rise, but Adam again forestalled her, his gold eyes flashing a firm but gentle warning.

After he filled two mugs with coffee and set them on the table, he pulled up a chair next to hers. 'I think it's time for me to listen,' he said softly. 'Would you please tell me what this is all about?'

Paris glanced at the piece of paper sitting so innocently on the table, then she raised her eyes to meet his. The look of genuine concern she could see in his eyes melted the last of her resistance.

'I have no proof,' she began, 'but I have a feeling that the person or persons responsible for breaking in here and for tampering with my car are members of the basketball team.'

'Tampering with your car . . . ' Adam echoed, shock and anger evident in his tone now.

For the next half hour, Paris carefully and meticulously related to Adam all the incidents that had taken place since the start of the year. Adam said little, only stopping her occasionally to ask a question or verify a point. When she finished he sat for a time without speaking.

'First of all,' Adam began as he pushed back his chair and stood up. 'I'd like to apologize for the way I behaved that day in my uncle's office. From what you've told me, it appears I did jump to the wrong conclusions.'

Paris glanced up at him in surprise. She hadn't expected an apology, and the fact that Adam had given her one was disconcerting. It was enough that he'd listened so attentively to her explanation, and now that he knew the facts, he would have to endorse her recommendation to suspend the basketball players.

'That's not important now,' she said, hoping he wouldn't notice the flush she could feel creeping across her cheeks. 'What bothers me is that we have to suspend the players at all, especially when there seems to be such a lot riding on the team this year. It'll be a blow to the college as well as to the team, if they lose those players.'

'Paris.' Her heart kicked against her ribs at the way he spoke her name, but something in Adam's tone made her turn and look at him.

'Yes?' she answered, and watched as he ran a hand agitatedly through his hair. He returned to the chair he'd vacated only moments ago and sat down. Resting his elbows on his knees, he leaned forward and met her gaze. 'I can't suspend the players.'

Shock ricocheted through her at his words, but before she could form a protest, Adam brought a finger to her lips.

'I know what you're going to say,' he quickly went on, 'but, believe me, there's more to this than meets the eye. I can't explain right now, but I do know what I'm doing. I want you to give me some more time. I know it's a lot to ask, but please, will you just trust me on this one?'

The storm of protest died on her lips as Paris gazed into the eyes of the man before her. She could sense the turmoil in him and she could see the plea in the depths of his eyes, a plea she found she couldn't ignore.

Perhaps it was the fact that he hadn't ordered her, that he'd plainly and simply asked her, but strangely enough she discovered she was willing to grant his request.

'All right, I'll hold off — but only for a few days,' she told him and immediately saw the look of relief that came into his eyes. 'But something will have to be done before the big game next Saturday,' she added. 'Those players are ineligible, and if they play, the entire team could risk suspension.' She shook her head. 'I don't really know why I'm agreeing to do this . . . '

Adam covered her hand with his. 'For now, it's enough that you are,' he said, surprised and relieved that she was willing to cooperate.

As he'd listened to her a few

moments ago, a feeling of anger the like of which he'd never known before had sprung to life within him. But unless he wanted to jeopardize the investigation already in progress, his hands were tied. He'd had no choice but to veto her recommendation, and only the knowledge that by doing so, he was protecting her, made the whole thing palatable.

The anger and outrage he'd expected from her hadn't materialized — instead she'd offered him her trust. It was more than he deserved. After all she'd been through — the harassment, the anonymous telephone calls, the tampering with her car — it was a whole lot more than he had any right to ask.

9

'Are you sure I can't persuade you to come back to Lillian's with me, just for tonight?' Adam asked a short while later.

'Thank you, but I'll be fine,' Paris replied, warmed by his concern. 'And thanks again for all you've done,' she added as she walked with him to the front door. 'I guess I must have sounded a little demented on the phone.' She felt slightly embarrassed now, remembering how she'd shouted at him.

'You sounded frightened,' Adam replied easily. 'Which was understand-able under the circumstances.'

'Why were you calling me, anyway?' Paris asked.

'To apologize,' he said as he opened the door and turned to face her. 'It's becoming something of a habit,' he added, flashing her a teasing grin.

Paris couldn't stop the smile that came to her lips, nor could she do anything about the way her heart somersaulted in instant response.

They stared at each other for what seemed an eternity, and Paris found herself wishing Adam would close the gap between them and take her into his arms once more.

Adam stood in the doorway gazing into eyes as green as the ocean and twice as inviting. Though he longed to accept the invitation he could see in their depths, if he kissed her now, he doubted he'd have the strength or the willpower to walk away.

With a sigh, he reached out and gently grazed her cheek with his knuckles. 'Good night, Paris. I'll call you tomorrow,' he added, before striding off into the darkness.

Paris released the breath she hadn't known she'd been holding. Shutting the door, she leaned against it for support and put a tentative hand to her cheek where a tingling warmth lingered.

She'd seen the look of regret in Adam's eyes a fleeting second before he turned away, and she was more than a little taken aback by the feeling of disappointment she was still trying to combat.

Locking the door behind her, Paris slowly made her way upstairs. She undressed and slipped between the covers, but she knew sleep would be a long time coming. Arriving back to find there had been a break-in was distressing enough, but Adam's presence, and the sensations and emotions that sprang to life whenever he was near, were somehow far more disturbing to her peace of mind.

When he'd asked her to trust him, she'd readily agreed. Her response had been instinctive, coming straight from her heart, leaving her to face the realization that she believed he was worthy of that trust.

But how could she trust Adam after what he'd done to Francesca? The question rose up to haunt her and for the first time she began to wonder if the man she'd come to know was indeed the same man she believed was responsible for the pain and heartache Francesca had suffered.

She'd always considered herself to be a good judge of character, and all her instincts seemed to be telling her that Adam Kincaid was not the kind of man who used women and then discarded them.

Paris closed her eyes and instantly an image of Adam filled her mind. When he'd arrived at the doorstep a few hours ago looking anxious and pale, his concern had been solely for her. He'd made her feel safe and protected, just by being there.

He could easily have chosen to call the police and leave the matter in their hands. But he hadn't. He'd come halfway across town just to make sure she was all right. That wasn't the action of a man who didn't care about anything or anyone.

But hadn't he abandoned Francesca at a time when she'd needed him most? Paris reminded herself, fighting now with her conscience. But hard though she tried, she couldn't seem to reignite those old feelings of anger and resentment.

And suddenly she recalled the conversation she'd had with Adam when she'd accused him of jumping to the wrong conclusions. He'd implied she was guilty of the same offense. Was he right?

The question played inside her head like a broken record, and for the second time in as many minutes, Paris found herself wondering if she had misjudged Adam.

But if Adam wasn't to blame, then the only other explanation was that Francesca had lied. It was something Paris had never considered before, and the feelings of guilt that accompanied the thought were upsetting indeed.

She'd adored Francesca and been more than a little in awe of her cousin who'd seemed so grown-up, so adult and so beautiful. Had she perhaps been blinded by that adoration, unable and unwilling to see any flaws?

Francesca had been a girl of eighteen at the time, young and immature in many ways. The more Paris explored the notion, the more she began to realize that the picture she'd always seen as black and white had a number of gray areas she hadn't noticed before.

Suddenly she longed to talk to Adam, to ask all the questions buzzing inside her head. But she doubted he'd be willing to answer them, especially when she'd already proclaimed his guilt.

Had she been wrong? It was a question that kept her awake for most of the night.

* * *

The next morning as Paris drove to the college, she tried to push all thoughts of Adam and Francesca aside. She was due to teach the senior class, and as she headed to the classroom the thought of seeing Jason French, Rick Diamond and Barry Kralic brought feelings of anger rising up inside her.

Which one of them had broken into her house? she wondered, as a group of students began to file in. And which one had written the threatening note? She knew that to confront them would be futile and her best course of action was to pretend nothing had happened, but during her hour-long lecture, she watched the smug and knowing glances pass between them, and found it increasingly difficult to contain her anger.

When the bell signifying the end of class rang out, Jason French was the first to stand up and head for the door.

'Wait a moment, please!' Paris called out above the noise of books closing and feet shuffling. 'The announcement I'm about to make applies only to Jason, Rick and Barry.' At these words the other students continued to pack up their belongings, though the noise remained at a lower level. 'With regard to the assignments the three of you were supposed to hand in last Friday, I'm extending the deadline to Thursday afternoon. If your papers are not in my office by three, I will be forced to take action. That's all, thank you.'

Paris let her glance skip to each of the students in turn and she saw them exchange questioning looks. With a nonchalance she was far from feeling, she busied herself rearranging her notes and putting them back in her file folder. To her relief, when she finally glanced up, the classroom was empty.

By late afternoon Paris returned to her office tired and tense. Leaning back in her chair, she stretched her hands above her head, trying to loosen muscles that were aching. She gazed outside at the descending darkness and for the first time since she'd moved to Brockton, the thought of driving home didn't bring the usual feeling of pleasure.

Though she knew it was unlikely that

the intruders had paid her another visit, she was reluctant to go home. She'd thought of inviting Lucy to dinner, just so she wouldn't have to enter the house on her own, but at lunchtime Lucy had been chattering about going to a show with her boyfriend. There was no one else she could ask. Except Adam.

She shook her head. What on earth had prompted her to think of Adam? She couldn't call him. He'd done more than enough already, coming all the way across town last night, just to make sure she was all right.

Silently, she chastised herself for her foolishness. She would drive home, light the fire and curl up with . . . the assignments she had to grade by the end of the week. Paris sighed, but still she made no move to rise from her chair.

The sharp knock on her office door startled her and she glanced up to see Adam framed in the doorway.

'I thought you might still be here,' he said as he crossed to her desk.

'Actually I was just about to leave,' Paris replied, trying to ignore the way her heart seemed to be dancing for joy at the sight of him.

'Then my timing's perfect,' Adam went on. 'I made the reservation for six, and it's nearly that now.'

'Reservation?' Paris repeated, frowning now, as she fought to regain control of her scattered senses.

'You're having dinner with me at the Faculty Club. Didn't I tell you?' he asked as his handsome face crinkled into a teasing smile.

'No, you didn't tell me,' Paris replied, but she was having difficulty trying to sound either angry or annoyed.

'I thought I just did,' came the quick reply, his smile widening.

'Adam, it's very kind of you, but — ' she began.

'No arguments,' he quickly cut in. 'Correct me if I'm wrong, but after what happened last night, I didn't think you'd be anxious to go home. And besides, I owe you a dinner, remember?'

206

His eyes held hers for a long moment, and seeing the look of tender concern, Paris found she didn't have the strength or the inclination to argue. Having dinner with Adam was infinitely more appealing than driving home to an empty house.

'Thanks, I'd like that,' she said, and at her words she saw something flicker briefly in the depths of his eyes.

The Faculty Club was a lounge and restaurant for the private use of college staff, their immediate families and any guests they might wish to entertain. The restaurant and lounge was located on the top floor of the administration building and afforded a panoramic view of Brockton.

Paris had never eaten at the club before but she'd heard a great deal about the food and how well the restaurant was run.

They didn't speak as they rode the elevator to the top floor, but Paris was conscious all the while of the man standing nearby. Glancing down at her ultrasuede shirtdress the color of cinnamon and the paisley scarf tied in a fluffy bow around her neck, she wished she'd chosen to wear something less business-like that morning. Adam, as always, looked immaculate in a dark camel-colored sports jacket, a vanilla shirt and rust tie, and brown slacks that hugged his muscular thighs.

When they arrived at the restaurant, Adam held the door for her and once inside, she was immediately drawn to the enormous fireplace at one end of the spacious room. Flames flickered a welcome, their warmth reaching out to curl around them and pull them farther into the room.

She noticed a number of familiar faces and acknowledged several greetings. The maître d' led them to a table by the window, and as he lit the tall candle inside the elegant centerpiece, Paris firmly reminded herself that she had accepted Adam's invitation simply because she hadn't been looking forward to going home.

'Have you eaten here before?' Adam asked, glancing up from the leather-bound menu before him.

Paris brought her eyes to meet his. 'Actually, no,' she replied, as her heartbeat began to accelerate once more.

'Do you like seafood?'

'Yes.'

'And pasta?'

'Yes,' she said, unable to stop the smile curling at the corners of her mouth.

'Then I'd recommend the seafood linguine. It's the best in town.'

'Sounds wonderful,' she replied as she closed the menu, disconcerted and charmed by the fact that he'd guessed she had a passion for pasta.

The waiter appeared moments later to take their order. 'Would you care for a glass of wine?' Adam asked.

'I'd prefer a Perrier, please,' she replied. When they were alone once more, Adam put his forearms on the table and leaned toward her.

'I have a small request to make,' he said, his tone even, his expression serious.

'What kind of request?' she asked, her heart sinking.

'Do you think that for the next few hours we could forget about the college . . . forget about the past and pretend that we've only just met?'

Of all the things she'd expected him to say, this request caught her completely off guard. She met and held his gaze for a long moment, and suddenly she felt something stir deep inside her. She lowered her eyes and focused on her hands, clasped on the table in front of her.

'All right,' she said, and at her words she saw the tension leave him.

She wasn't altogether sure why she'd agreed, but now that she'd made the decision, she felt somehow lighthearted and happier than she'd done in days.

'My name is Adam Kincaid,' Adam said with polite formality, but Paris saw the hint of humor in his eyes. 'I'm pleased to meet you,' he went on as he extended his hand across the table.

Paris hesitated, but only for a moment, unable to resist the smile hovering on the edge of his mouth. 'Paris Ford. I'm pleased to meet you, too,' she replied, keeping her tone light.

Adam's hand immediately engulfed hers and at his touch, a jolt of awareness made a lightning trip up her arm. She withdrew her hand instantly, and reaching for the large white napkin, she unfolded it and placed it on her lap, hoping against hope Adam hadn't noticed her reaction.

'Tell me about your family,' Adam said, breaking the rather tense silence. When she lifted her eyes to meet his, she was relieved to see that he showed no sign of having been aware of her reaction.

'My father was a construction engineer,' she told him. 'He died five years ago from a heart attack.'

'I'm sorry,' Adam said softly, his voice full of sympathy and regret.

Paris managed a tentative smile in

acknowledgment. 'My mother taught elementary school up until I was born,' she went on. 'She recently remarried, and now she and my stepfather live in Hawaii.'

'You were there for Christmas,' Adam said.

'That's right,' she answered, strangely pleased that he'd remembered. 'Now it's your turn,' she said, beginning to relax. 'Tell me about your family.'

Adam was silent for a moment, a thoughtful expression on his face. 'I don't remember my father very well. He died in a car accident when I was four. My mother was Uncle George's youngest sister, and she never recovered from my father's death. We lived in San Diego, where my mother worked as an assistant to a librarian. I used to come to Brockton for a month every summer. I loved it here,' he said with sincerity. 'George and Lillian were wonderful to me, and when my mother died, they offered me a home here, with them.'

The waiter arrived with two glasses of

Perrier, and departed once more.

'How old were you when your mother died?' Paris asked, after taking a sip of the sparkling liquid.

'Eleven,' Adam answered.

Paris felt tears prick her eyes as a wave of sympathy washed over her. Her heart ached for him and the pain of losing his parents at such a young age.

'Don't look so sad,' Adam said, seeing the moisture gathering in her eyes, making them shine like precious jewels. 'Lillian and George are my family, now. I've really been very lucky.'

Adam hadn't expected her to accept his invitation to dinner, but he was inordinately pleased that she had. Seeing her sitting across from him, looking as beautiful as a sunny spring morning, was doing strange things to his heart.

When she'd agreed to forget their differences, at least for a few hours, he'd felt as though he'd been given a second chance — a chance he didn't intend to throw away.

She was easy to talk to, as well as being a sympathetic listener, but he guessed that her innate shyness and air of fragile innocence made her the kind of woman men tended to overlook. But Adam sensed that beneath the surface Paris was a sensuous woman just waiting to be awakened, just waiting for the right man.

Dinner, when it came, was as delicious as Adam had promised. As they ate and talked, smiled and laughed, Paris found herself hanging on his every word. To her surprise, she discovered that they both liked watching Humphrey Bogart movies and reading fast-paced detective novels.

He was fun to be with, attentive and amusing, and as the minutes flew by, she began to wish the evening would never end.

When the waiter brought their coffee, Paris was startled to discover just how late it was.

'I'll follow you home and make sure there are no surprises waiting for you there,' Adam said as they walked back to the parking lot.

Paris happily accepted his offer, warmed once more by his thoughtfulness, and as she drove home it was somehow comforting to glance in the rearview mirror and see Adam's headlights right behind her.

At the house, everything appeared to be in order, but Adam insisted on taking a quick tour of the rooms just to make sure. 'Lock up after I'm gone,' he cautioned as he turned to leave.

'Thanks for everything,' Paris said, trying to convince herself that she wasn't disappointed when he made no move to kiss her good-night. But as she watched him walk to his car she found herself wondering anew at the emotions he aroused in her.

★ ★ ★

The next few days passed uneventfully for Paris. There were no anonymous telephone calls in the middle of the night, and she had no more problems with her car.

Adam called the morning after they'd had dinner together, but his call was brief and he made no mention of the students, nor did he say anything about what action he planned to take. All she could assume was that he had some plan in the offing. She had agreed to wait, to trust him, and she would do just that, but as the weekend approached, she was becoming increasingly impatient to have the situation resolved.

If action wasn't taken and the three players were allowed to play, the basketball program at Brockton would be in jeopardy. As far as she was concerned, rules were meant to be kept, especially when breaking them could mean disqualification of the team and embarrassment and humiliation for the college.

By Thursday afternoon, her patience was fast running out. The day of the basketball game was drawing nearer, and as the general air of excitement began to build throughout the student body and the faculty, Paris became more and more uneasy.

Though she held out little hope of the senior students handing in their assignments as she'd asked, she waited in her office just in case.

Anger and annoyance stirred to life within her as the deadline came and went. At four o'clock, she closed up her office and crossed the campus to the administration building. She'd decided to go and see Adam and ask what he planned to do. Surely she'd given him enough time?

As the elevator doors slid open at the fifth floor she was surprised to note that the outer office area was deserted. Had Adam left? she wondered as she made her way down the carpeted hall.

She'd only taken two steps when she heard the sound of voices coming from Adam's office. She slowed to a halt. Perhaps she should wait.

Suddenly the door to his office opened, and Paris froze as the sound of Stuart Unger's voice drifted toward her.

'And everything is taken care of?' she heard Stuart Unger ask.

'Everything,' came Adam's reply.

'Good,' Unger continued in a satisfied tone. 'You know how important this game is, I wouldn't want anything to go wrong.'

'What could go wrong?' Adam asked. 'Come on, I'll buy you a beer,' he added, his tone warm and friendly.

Listening to the brief exchange, Paris felt a cold chill chase down her spine and a sharp pain stab at her heart. Her next action was instinctive. Reaching for the handle of the nearest office door, she quickly ducked inside, praying silently that no one was there.

To her relief, the room was empty. She held her breath, waiting for them to leave. Seconds later, the muffled sound of voices reached her, followed by the heavy tread of footsteps as they strode past her hiding place.

Paris slowly released the breath she'd been holding and leaned against the door, biting down on her lower lip to stop the moan of protest threatening to escape.

Adam had lied to her! Deliberately lied! It was all she could think about, and the pain that accompanied the thought was almost more than she could stand.

When he'd asked her to trust him, he'd simply been buying time — he'd had no intention of taking any action against the players. And most likely his invitation to dinner had merely been all part of his plan to keep her from taking action. There was no plan as she'd thought, and like a fool she'd let herself be drawn in by his charm, falling under his spell just as Francesca had done.

Tears filled her eyes and a fresh pain ricocheted through her, leaving her to wonder why she should suddenly feel as though someone had torn her heart from her body.

Fool! she silently chided herself, facing the knowledge that somewhere deep in her heart she had begun to believe she might have misjudged him and the role he'd played in Francesca's life twelve years ago.

But not any longer. Anger came to her rescue, and as the emotion steadily gathered strength within her, it helped to dampen some of the pain.

The sound of the elevator arriving on the floor broke into her thoughts, and taking a deep breath, Paris opened the door a crack. Though she wasn't sure what had prompted her to hide, she was glad now she hadn't had to face Adam or Unger.

Slowly now, she slipped from the office. Instead of taking the elevator, she opted for the stairs, wanting to give them ample time to leave the campus.

When at last she reached the parking lot, she was relieved to see that Adam's car had gone. Throughout the drive home, Paris tried to keep thoughts of Adam and his betrayal of her trust at bay, but she found the task both painful and difficult. By the time she pulled into her driveway, the ache in her heart had returned a thousandfold.

10

Paris spent the night tossing and turning as images of Adam and Unger drifted through her dreams. She dreamt she'd arrived at the game with all eight members of the board of directors in tow. But instead of stopping the game and suspending the players, the board members proceeded to cheer and clap and encourage the team, while she stood on the sidelines feeling like a fool.

In her dream, she noticed that Unger and Adam were also participating in the game, but to her surprise, they appeared to be on opposing teams.

When Adam spotted her, she'd hurried outside, only to have him chase after her. She hadn't gone far when he caught her, turning her around to stare at her accusingly, a look of pain in the depths of his eyes.

Paris awoke in a tangle of sheets with

the vivid image of the reproachful and hurt expression she'd seen on Adam's face etched in her mind.

She lay awake for the remainder of the night, her thoughts and emotions in a turmoil. By the time her alarm clock signified the start of the day, she'd made the decision to call the administration offices and set up a meeting with the college board of directors.

She felt duty-bound to report all that had been happening with the students, and, if necessary, to explain why she hadn't taken the matter up with Adam Kincaid, acting athletic director.

When she arrived at the college, she immediately put the call through to the academic office.

'This is Miss Ford from the English department,' she told the secretary who answered. 'I'd like to make an appointment to see the board.'

'Today?' came the surprised response.

'Yes. It's urgent,' Paris replied, impatience edging her tone.

'This is rather short notice,' said the

woman curtly. 'Several members of the board are unavailable today. Couldn't this wait until Monday?'

'No, it can't wait,' Paris answered, trying to keep her anger in check.

'I see,' said the secretary, after a lengthy pause. 'In that case I'll contact the members who are available and call you back.'

Throughout the morning, Paris tried to concentrate on the lessons and lectures she had prepared for her classes. Not until she returned to her office during the lunch break did she receive confirmation that a meeting with five of the board members had been scheduled for three o'clock that afternoon.

With no classes to teach that afternoon, Paris busied herself marking papers, but she found her concentration continuously wandering from the task. More than once, she reached for the telephone, her intention to call Adam. But then she'd remember the conversation she'd overheard with Unger and she'd replace the receiver, telling herself she wasn't under any obligation to let Adam know what action she was taking.

But somehow she couldn't forget the kindness and concern he'd shown her after the break-in. Nor could she forget the evening they'd spent at the Faculty Club. Those and other memories lingered on the edges of her mind, arousing emotions she wished she didn't feel, and making it impossible for her to keep thoughts of Adam at bay.

With a groan of disgust, Paris tossed the papers she'd been attempting to read onto the pile on her desk and stood up. She glanced at the clock. It was only two-fifteen, and suddenly she wished her interview was over and the matter was out of her hands.

Gathering up several files from the basket on her desk, she crossed to the filing cabinet. Just as she opened the drawer the telephone rang. Sighing, she returned to her desk and picked up the receiver.

'Hello!'

'Miss Ford? Stuart Unger here,' said the familiar voice and Paris felt the hairs on the back of her neck prickle in warning.

'Mr. Unger,' she acknowledged, keeping her tone even.

'I was wondering if you could stop by my office for a few minutes,' he said, his tone friendly.

'I have an appointment a little later this afternoon,' Paris said. 'Is it important?'

'Yes,' Unger replied. 'I've come up with an idea on how to solve the problem you've been having with my star basketball players.'

'Isn't it a little late for quick solutions?' Paris asked, unable to hide her surprise. She wondered fleetingly if somehow he'd learned of her impending meeting with the board.

'Better late than never, as the saying goes,' came his prompt reply, his tone jovial and full of confidence.

'I'm sorry, but I really don't . . . ' she began.

'Please,' he cut in, his tone coaxing now. 'I know we haven't exactly seen eye to eye on this, but I think I've found a way to work out our differences.'

Paris hesitated. Wasn't this what she'd been hoping for from the start? Surely there wouldn't be any harm in listening to what he had to say? 'All right,' she relented. 'I'll be right over.'

'Thank you. You won't regret it,' he added, relief evident in his voice. 'Oh, by the way, I've had to move out of my office. It's being recarpeted. I've set up a temporary office in the old locker rooms below the gym.'

'How do I find them?' she asked.

'When you come in the main entrance, turn to your right and go through the first set of doors. The stairs there lead down to the old locker rooms. You can't miss them,' Unger assured her. 'I really appreciate this, Miss Ford, thank you,' he added, a hint of sarcasm in his voice now, but before she could say more, he hung up.

Frowning, Paris replaced the receiver

and glanced up at the clock. It was already twenty minutes past two. She'd give him ten minutes, no more, she thought as she gathered up the three files she'd need later at her meeting with the board. Grabbing her coat and purse, she headed for the door.

A blustery wind whipped around her as she hurried across campus, but her thoughts were on Stuart Unger. His sudden friendliness seemed strangely out of character, especially when he'd made it obvious from the outset that he considered her nothing more than a nuisance. What had prompted the change? she wondered.

When she reached the gymnasium, the door was opened from the inside. 'Hello, Miss Ford.'

Paris glanced at the student and smiled when she saw Neil Pavan. 'Hi, Neil,' she responded. 'Thanks,' she added as she slipped inside, and he continued on his way.

Glad to be out of the cold, Paris followed Unger's directions, anxious now to find out what he had to say. At the foot of the stairs, there stretched before her a corridor with several doors leading from it.

The smell of mildew filled the air as she made her way toward the doorway, and she couldn't help thinking that Unger could have picked a better place for a temporary office. It was decidedly cold beneath the gym and a ripple of unease chased down her spine, making her wish she hadn't agreed to come.

'There you are,' Stuart Unger said as he appeared in one of the doorways.

'I should have suggested that you come to my office instead of meeting here,' Paris said as she reached him.

'But that would have spoiled my surprise,' he replied with a smile that sent fresh shivers of alarm running through her.

'Surprise?' she repeated, as Unger moved aside to let her enter. Paris moved cautiously into the room and came to a halt. There was no desk, no sign of anything that would indicate that this room was being used as an office.

'What the . . . ' she began, but before she could say more, she felt Unger's hand on her back, and suddenly she was propelled forcefully into the room.

The files and her purse tumbled unheeded to the floor as Paris instinctively reached out to stop herself from crashing into the row of metal lockers that seemed to be rushing straight toward her.

She let out a cry of pain as her hands smacked against the lockers, effectively knocking the breath out of her. Slightly dazed from the impact, she turned to see Unger standing in the open doorway, his eyes burning with hatred, the friendly façade a thing of the past.

'You couldn't take a hint and mind your own business, could you?' he said, anger and bitterness tainting every word. 'Lucky for me, I asked the secretary over at the administration office to let me know if you made an appointment with the directors. I can't have you spoiling everything . . . not now . . . ' He started to close the door.

'Wait! You're not going to leave me here?' Paris said disbelievingly.

Unger laughed, a sound that sent a shudder through her. 'Don't look so worried, someone will find you . . . eventually.'

'No . . . wait . . . please . . . ' Paris pleaded, as she stumbled across the room toward him. She reached the door in time to hear the key being turned in the lock.

* * *

Adam frowned as he replaced the telephone receiver. Where was she? When he asked Marjorie to find out when Paris would be finished for the day, she'd informed him Paris had no classes on Friday afternoon. But she wasn't in her office; he'd just tried to call her.

She hadn't gone home, because he'd seen her car in the parking lot when he'd returned from his meeting in town a short while ago.

Adam glanced at his watch again. It was almost three-thirty. Where was she?

Other than a brief phone call on the morning following their dinner together, he'd been enmeshed in so many meetings and negotiations that he hadn't had time to call her again.

The reason he'd hurried back to the campus today was to see her, to tell her what he'd wanted to tell her the night of the break-in — that Stuart Unger was under investigation.

But until this afternoon, he hadn't been able to convince Detectives Cooper and Johnston that if they didn't give him permission to tell Paris what was going on, she might well take matters into her own hands and jeopardize the entire investigation.

That had convinced them — but now that he had their approval, she was nowhere to be found.

Perhaps he'd missed seeing her heading to her car and she was already at home, he thought, as he reached for the telephone and dialed her number. But after listening to the phone ring six times, Adam slammed down the receiver and ran a hand agitatedly through his hair.

Leaning back in his chair, he let his thoughts drift back to Sunday evening — the night of the break-in. He recalled quite vividly the feeling of fear that had clutched at his insides when he'd heard her shouting hysterically at him over the phone. And during the drive across town, he'd repeatedly had to talk to himself, to try and calm the rage running rampant through him.

The feeling of relief that had washed over him when he saw her standing in the doorway of the house was something he wouldn't soon forget.

For an insane moment, he'd wanted simply to haul her into his arms, to feel her body next to his, just to assure himself that she was all right. It had taken some effort on his part not to give in to the urge, especially when he saw the look of fear lingering in the depths of her lovely green eyes.

The moment he'd read the threatening note, his anger had swiftly risen to the surface again, but it had quickly been replaced by the overwhelming need to protect this woman, and to protect her with his life.

Later as he'd listened to her relate the incidents prior to the break-in, he'd silently berated himself for the way he'd handled the situation when she'd first approached him.

He should have realized at the outset that she wasn't the kind of teacher who ran to the administration with minor problems. He'd had a number of important things on his mind at the time, though, including his uncle's heart attack.

But she'd made a lasting impression with those challenging green eyes. Never before had he met a woman who'd aroused his emotions quite so quickly or so strongly. In a very short space of time, Paris had gently nudged her way into his heart, creating a distraction he could well do without.

Each time he'd seen her, he'd grown more and more fascinated by her air of innocence. And each time he'd kissed her, he'd found it increasingly difficult to ignore the passion that exploded between them.

But fate had dealt him a tough hand, he reminded himself, and a sigh of frustration escaped as his thoughts turned now to Paris's cousin, Francesca. Would Paris be willing to listen to the truth? he wondered. He'd been tempted to bring up the topic of Francesca the night he'd taken Paris to the Faculty Club. But he'd been the one to make the request that they put their differences aside for a few hours, and when she'd agreed, he hadn't wanted to spoil what for him had been one of the most memorable evenings of his life.

He was sure they'd taken a step toward friendship that night, but he knew, too, that as long as the past lay between them, it was unlikely he could hope for a deeper, more lasting relationship.

He needed to talk to her about Francesca, about Unger, but first things first — he had to find her. Where was she?

*　*　*

'Let me out! Somebody, please! Let me out!' Paris yelled, as she hammered on the locker-room door. Her hand was throbbing painfully now and her throat felt raw from all the shouting she'd been doing.

She glanced at her watch for what must have been the hundredth time, and moaned in despair. It was three-thirty. She'd only been in the locker-room for an hour, but somehow it felt more like six.

At first she'd thought it would only be a matter of time before someone started looking for her. Surely when she didn't show up for her appointment with the board, the secretary would immediately know something was amiss.

But as the minutes ticked by, Paris was forced to face the possibility that no one was even aware that she was missing.

Tears welled up in her eyes and a knot of tension tightened inside her chest. Unger had said he couldn't let her spoil everything. What had he meant by that? she wondered. And how long would it be before someone realized she was missing?

Outside, it was already beginning to get dark, and as usual on Friday afternoon, students and faculty alike would soon be leaving to go home.

Paris let her gaze drift to the row of narrow windows, made from frosted glass, high up on the opposite wall. She couldn't see out and she doubted anyone could see in, and even if she managed to climb on top of the lockers, she knew she still wouldn't be able to reach the windows.

With a sigh, Paris crossed to the bench in front of the metal lockers and sat down. Moments after Unger closed the door, she'd explored every corner of the locker room, as well as the adjoining shower room and bathrooms, making the discovery that the only way out was through the door Unger had locked.

His call saying he had a solution to her problem had been a ploy to get her to the locker room, and like a fool she'd fallen for it.

Paris pulled her coat around her and silently berated herself for being taken in so easily. She'd sensed instinctively Unger wasn't man she could trust, and his complete change of attitude should have alerted her that something was wrong. After he'd locked her in, he'd probably put a call through to the board office and canceled her appointment, she thought frustratedly.

Why hadn't she told someone what she'd planned to do? How she wished she'd called Adam. If she had, he might be looking for her ... or at least wondering about her.

Annoyed with herself, Paris rose from the bench, and thrusting her hands deep into the pockets of her quilted raincoat, she began to pace the room.

When she turned toward the locker, she spotted a tube of lipstick which she guessed had fallen from her purse and rolled under the wooden bench. She bent to retrieve it, and as she put the lipstick away, she suddenly remembered the chocolate bar she'd bought the day before. Rummaging through her purse, she located it, triumphantly raising it above her head as if it were a bar of gold.

'I guess I won't starve to death,' she said aloud. 'Or will I?' she added, hating herself for the despair she could hear creeping into her voice.

'Stop it!' she chided herself, and with a determined effort, she fought down the panic threatening to overwhelm her, repeatedly telling herself it was only a matter of time before someone realized she was missing — until someone spotted her car in the parking lot and started to look for her.

Another hour passed, an hour that seemed endless, an hour that left her feeling chilled to the bone and fighting off depression once again. But it was increasingly difficult to keep her spirits up, when with each passing minute, the odds of anyone finding her before morning were rapidly diminishing.

To cheer herself a little she unwrapped the chocolate bar and took several small bites, chewing slowly, savoring every morsel, trying to make it last. Tempted though she was, she refrained from eating all of it, carefully rewrapping the bar before returning it to her purse.

She rose and began to pace the room once more, this time focusing her thoughts on Unger, trying to fathom just why the threat of having the three players suspended from the basketball team would have prompted him to take such drastic action.

From the bitter words he'd flung at her before he'd locked her in, she guessed he'd had something to do with the threatening note she'd found the night of the break-in. The more she thought about it, the more she was convinced that Unger must have had a hand in everything; from the anonymous telephone calls to tampering with her car.

In a subtle, yet determined way, he'd been trying to intimidate her, hoping to frighten her into handing out the passing grades his players needed. Suddenly Paris remembered Unger saying he wished she was more like her predecessor, Mrs. Wilkinson. Had Mrs. Wilkinson taken early retirement because of Unger's intimidation tactics?

Paris brought her thoughts to a halt, her head spinning with questions she couldn't answer. It was all speculation, of course, she had no proof. All she was really sure of was that he'd enticed her to the locker rooms and imprisoned her there, just to prevent his players from being suspended. But why was this game so important?

Suddenly Paris found her thoughts

shifting to Adam and to the night of the break-in. He'd told her there was more to the problem than she knew — had he known Unger was involved in something even then? But why hadn't Adam told her? A thought struck her — because he didn't have proof — and perhaps he hadn't told her because he'd been trying to protect her.

But what about the conversation she'd overheard between Adam and Unger? They'd been chatting about the game like two friends, and because she'd gone to ask Adam what he intended to do about the three students, she'd assumed when she heard them that he was somehow involved with Unger.

Had she misunderstood or misinterpreted what she'd heard? Had Adam been trying to get close to Unger in the hope of finding out what he was up to? On reflection, the conversation she'd overheard had been quite innocent. Had she jumped to the wrong conclusions? Adam had accused her of that before. Was he right?

With a sinking heart, Paris knew that that was exactly what she'd done. Adam wasn't in any way involved with Unger, because the Adam Kincaid she'd come to know in the past few weeks wasn't the kind of man who'd risk his career or jeopardize the integrity of Brockton College.

Adam was a generous and caring man, a man who put other people's needs before his own. It was a quality he'd demonstrated more than once since he'd arrived in Brockton. Whatever he'd done, it had been in the best interests of the college.

And all at once Paris realized with startling clarity that she'd been wrong about Adam from the start. He hadn't abandoned Francesca ... he was incapable of abandoning anyone in need of help. And whatever happened twelve years ago, he, like Francesca, had been a victim.

Feelings of guilt and remorse washed over her, leaving in their wake an aching heart. Right from the moment she'd set eyes on Adam again, she'd been fighting her attraction for him.

Wanting to deny her feelings, wanting to keep him at a distance, she'd repeatedly reminded herself of his involvement with her cousin, Francesca. But her heart had known better — her heart had struggled to tell her she was wrong about him, and she wished now she'd had the courage to listen.

Suddenly, she was filled with a longing to see Adam, to tell him she was sorry, and to ask his forgiveness. But she knew that if he couldn't find it in his heart to give her another chance, she only had herself to blame.

A searing pain, the like of which she'd never felt before, tore through her, bringing a moan of anguish to her lips, forcing her to face what she'd known in her heart for days, but refused to acknowledge. She was irrevocably and completely in love with Adam Kincaid.

11

Paris rolled onto her side, trying to find a comfortable position on the hard wooden bench, but it was impossible.

Using her purse as a pillow, she huddled inside her raincoat and closed her eyes, shutting out the glaring neon lights high above her.

She'd switched them off earlier, but sitting in the eerie darkness had been even more frightening, and so she'd turned them on again.

She was exhausted, both mentally and physically, but much as she would have preferred to sleep away some of the hours till morning, she was too cold to relax and too keyed up to unwind.

Was anyone looking for her? she wondered. Was Adam? The idea that he might be searching for her brought a plethora of emotions to the surface, but she quickly reminded herself that it was unlikely Adam, or anyone, even knew she was missing.

She hadn't told anyone about her meeting with Unger, and other than the secretary at the administration office, no one had known of her meeting with the board — only Unger, she thought ironically.

And if her car remained in the parking lot overnight, it could easily be explained — she'd taken a taxi or been given a ride home.

She'd had no specific plans for the weekend, no prior arrangements, no dinner engagement. Therefore, there was no reason at all for anyone to wonder where she might be . . . or to check up on her, at least until Monday, when she didn't show up for work.

The thought of being stranded in the locker room for two more nights brought a shudder of alarm racing through her, but Paris firmly refused to give up hope and shifted her thoughts in another direction.

What about Adam? There was a

slight chance he might have tried to contact her. Her heart turned over at the idea, picking up speed and successfully lifting her spirits several notches.

She let her mind fill with an image of him, his thick brown hair, his gold-speckled eyes, his strong jawline, that sensuous mouth, and slowly she drifted off into a fantasy world, a world where she saw Adam astride a beautiful white stallion, galloping across a field toward her.

She smiled to herself, enjoying the fantasy, wishing indeed it was true and at any moment he would come bursting through the door to take her in his arms.

Paris held her breath, listening eagerly for a sound that would tell her she was soon to be rescued, but all she could hear was her heart thundering against her rib cage, like a herd of stampeding horses.

Paris drifted in and out of consciousness for the remainder of the night, finding comfort in her dreams, dreams in which Adam played a prominent role.

When she awoke her body ached from top to toe, making her wonder if the horses in her dreams had, in fact, run over her.

Groaning in protest with every step, she crossed to the shower room and bathrooms and gazed longingly at the shower stalls. All she'd been able to get from the bathroom taps the previous evening had been a slow trickle of icy cold water, so she had to content herself now with washing her face and hands.

Feeling a little more refreshed, she wandered back into the locker room and for breakfast, ate half of the remainder of the chocolate bar.

Throughout the morning, she engaged in a number of activities. She lost count of the number of times she walked the length of the room and as she paced, she sang the words of every song she ever knew. And when she ran out of songs, she played mental games in an attempt to keep her thoughts away from the nagging fear lurking on the outskirts of her mind — that she might never be found.

Adam was never far from her thoughts. There was both pleasure and pain in the knowledge that she loved him, and with each passing minute her longing to tell him of her feelings intensified.

She thought about Francesca, wishing now she hadn't lost touch with her cousin, and wondering if she would ever learn the truth about what happened twelve years ago.

But as the afternoon hours passed, she had to continually fight off the feeling of panic that threatened to overwhelm her, whenever she thought of having to spend another night in the locker room.

She sat down on the hard wooden bench and turned her thoughts to her mother and stepfather in Hawaii, wishing she was with them, wishing she could hug them both and tell them how much she loved them. But instead of lifting her spirits, these thoughts only served to dampen them more.

With a moan of despair, Paris lay down on the hard wooden bench and tried to swallow the emotion suddenly clogging her throat. Closing her eyes, she felt hot tears slip from beneath her lashes.

All at once, a strange noise startled the silence. Her eyes flew open and she sat up, straining to catch the sound again.

Suddenly she heard a muffled sound coming from the corridor — or was it coming from above? Paris glanced at her watch, noting it was past three o'clock. The basketball game was scheduled to start at five. Perhaps she was simply hearing a few fans arriving.

Hopping off the bench, Paris crossed to the door and listened once more. The noise came again, but much closer . . . someone was outside in the corridor. Paris immediately began yelling at the top of her voice.

'I'm in here! Help me! Please, help me!'

'Paris? Paris, is that you?' There was no mistaking Adam's deep voice and hearing it, Paris had to bite down on her lower lip to stifle the sob that rose in her throat.

'Adam? Yes . . . it's me,' she said brokenly, swallowing the tears threatening to choke her.

'Thank God!' Adam said, relief evident in his tone. 'Are you all right?' he asked anxiously.

'I'm fine . . . now,' she said, suddenly feeling weak all over.

'I'll have you out in a minute,' he assured her. 'I know where there's a key. I'll be right back.'

'Please, hurry,' Paris said softly, fighting once more to hold back tears.

Five, long agonizing minutes passed before Adam returned and she heard the wonderful sound of a key being turned in the lock. When the door opened, she was suddenly crushed against his tall frame, scarcely able to breathe, but she didn't mind in the least. Shivering with reaction, she clung to him and let the tears flow.

'It's all right, my love,' Adam murmured against her hair. 'You're safe. I've got you. I've got you.'

Paris couldn't let go, afraid he would vanish, but his warmth and strength soon chased away the last of her fear, and the last of her despair.

Taking a steadying breath, she drew away to look up into his eyes. 'How did you find me?' she asked.

'Luck, and a little guesswork,' he said with a shaky laugh, before he kissed her on her forehead. 'I've been looking for you since late yesterday,' he went on. 'No one seemed to know where you were. I even drove out to your house last night, but there was no sign of you there. I came back here. I knew you had to be somewhere on campus.'

'Do you mean you've been looking for me all night?' she asked incredulously.

'All night,' Adam replied and the

lingering anxiety she could hear in his tone confirmed his words.

Glancing quickly over his features now, Paris noticed the lines of strain on his handsome face, as well as the hint of stubble on his chin, and her heart flip-flopped inside her breast at the knowledge that he'd spent the night looking for her.

'But what made you look here?' she asked.

'I ran into one of your students . . . Neil Pavan. He was on his way to the dressing room to get ready for the game. I just asked him if he'd seen you. He said he ran into you outside the gym, yesterday afternoon. It was all I had to go on,' he said evenly. 'I'm not sure why I thought of the old locker rooms . . . a hunch I guess. But it paid off . . . thank God,' he added gazing intently at her, drinking in the sight of her before hauling her against him once more.

For the past twenty-four hours, he'd been living a nightmare, pushed to the edge of sanity as his imagination supplied numerous scenarios of what had happened to Paris — each one worse than the last.

But the moment he heard her voice, the joy and relief that exploded through him were like fireworks going off on the Fourth of July, and in that moment, the emotion he'd been too afraid to acknowledge burst free, making itself known. He was in love with her . . . and the feeling was like nothing he'd ever known before. But much as he wanted to tell her, he knew this was neither the time nor the place. Besides, there was still some unfinished business to attend to . . .

'How did you end up down here . . . was it Unger?' he asked, focusing with some difficulty on the problem at hand.

Surprised, Paris drew away. 'Yes . . . he called and said he wanted to see me . . . but it was just a trick to get me here,' Paris said. At her words she felt Adam tense and saw his eyes darken in anger.

'When I get my hands on him, I'll . . . ' Adam muttered, his arms tightening protectively around her.

'No . . . wait . . . he's up to something, Adam. And it has to do with the game tonight. I was on my way to the board office to ask for the suspension of those players . . . '

'I should have guessed,' Adam cut in wryly, a faint smile curling at the corners of his mouth.

'I had to,' she responded. 'I couldn't wait any longer, not with the game coming up . . . '

'You did the right thing,' Adam assured her. 'I should have told you what was going on — then maybe none of this would have happened.'

'It wasn't your fault,' Paris quickly intervened, warmed by the fact that he felt he had to shoulder part of the blame. 'How could you guess what Unger would do? What I don't understand is why it was so important to stop those players from being suspended.'

'It must have something to do with the game tonight. Or maybe he found out he was under investigation . . . '

'Under investigation? Why?' Paris asked.

'Misappropriation of college funds,' came the reply, and she could only stare at Adam in astonishment. 'Not only that,' he continued, 'but the police have reason to believe he's involved with a gambling syndicate. As yet, they have no proof.'

'Gambling?' Paris said, shaking her head in disbelief.

'I think it's time I had a talk with Mr. Unger,' Adam said heatedly. 'The game doesn't start for another hour, but knowing Unger, he's probably up in his office working out his strategy. I think he'll be surprised to see you. Let's find out, shall we?'

There was more than a hint of violence in the depths of his eyes as he ushered Paris along the corridor and up the flight of stairs leading to the main floor. A number of people were milling around, but no one paid any attention to them as they made their way toward the mezzanine floor and Unger's office.

As they approached the stairs, a man wearing a brown overcoat atop a rumpled suit broke away from a small group of people and hurried toward them. 'You found her, I see,' he said as Adam slowed to a halt.

'I found her,' Adam acknowledged, his arm still around Paris. 'And now I'm going to have a little chat with Mr. Unger,' he continued. 'Why don't you come, too, Cooper — you might find it enlightening.'

'What do you have in mind, Adam?' the man asked.

'I'm playing it by ear,' Adam replied. 'Oh, by the way, Paris, this is Detective Cooper,' he said, as they began to climb the stairs.

When they reached the top, Paris noticed that the door to Unger's office was closed. Without bothering to knock, Adam flung the door wide-open, an action that brought the four occupants in the room to their feet.

Unger's look of surprise changed fleetingly to fear when he saw Paris standing in the doorway.

'Is this a private party, or can anyone join in?' Adam asked, his voice heavy with sarcasm.

Unger quickly turned to Adam. 'Hey . . . buddy . . . what gives?' he asked, and at the casual, friendly tone, Adam had to grit his teeth and fight down the sudden urge to climb over the desk and put his fist into the face of the man he'd once thought was his friend.

'I think it's time to cut the b.s., Stuart. You're in big trouble, and so are your cohorts here,' Adam said, turning now to the three students, staring white-faced at him. 'Let me see,' he continued, barely managing to keep his anger in check. 'You must be Jason French, Barry Kralic and Rick Diamond — am I right?'

Each student glanced nervously at Unger, obviously looking to him for direction.

'Have you met Detective Cooper?' Adam asked. 'He has a file on each of you. The charges run like this — breaking and entering, tampering with a car, threats, illegal betting . . . How am I doing?'

His question was met with a tension-filled silence. 'Oh, and don't think I've forgotten you, Stuart,' he added, turning back to Unger. 'We can start with misappropriation of college funds,' Adam continued, 'and what about unlawful confinement?'

Unger glanced at Paris and a look of rage crossed his features. Instinctively Paris shrank from the threat in his cold blue eyes. Adam reached out to take her hand, and feeling his strength and his warmth engulf her once more, she relaxed a little.

'We just did what he told us to do,' Jason French blurted out defiantly, breaking the silence.

'Shut up, you fool,' Unger ordered. 'He's just bluffing. They can't prove anything,' he said, but his voice trembled and lacked conviction.

'Dream on,' Adam said scornfully. 'What about tonight's little scam, Stuart? That's what this meeting is all about, isn't it?'

Standing next to Adam, Paris watched the scene play out before her, feeling strangely sorry now for the three young men.

'I don't know what you're talking about,' Unger said, but Paris could see the film of perspiration breaking out on Unger's forehead.

'What's so important about tonight's game?' Adam asked, hoping to goad one of the players into making an unguarded response, but no one spoke. 'Not that it matters,' he continued, 'because you're finished, Unger — you and your three friends here are on your way to prison.'

'No . . . not prison . . . ' Unger said, fear in his voice and a look of desperation on his face as all the bravado and confidence he'd shown moments ago vanished like air escaping from a balloon.

'I'm afraid Detective Cooper might argue with you on that,' Adam went on relentlessly. 'He has some questions for you, Stuart, concerning your involvement with a gambling syndicate . . . '

At these words, Unger's composure shattered completely and he sank into the chair behind the desk, dropping his head onto his hands.

Adam quickly turned his attention to the students. 'What was the plan, boys?' he asked casually.

There was silence for a long moment then Rick Diamond spoke. 'He wanted us to throw the game,' he said, defeat evident in his voice. 'He said there was a lot of money riding on it . . . '

'I'll take over now,' Detective Cooper said, stepping farther into the room and flashing Adam a look of admiration and gratitude.

'But what about the game? What's going to happen now?' This time it was Barry Kralic who spoke, and Paris heard regret as well as a hint of remorse in his voice.

'We'll just have to win, won't we?' Adam said confidently. 'Can you manage on your own now, Cooper?'

'No problem,' came the reply. 'Johnston should be waiting downstairs. Tell him to hightail it up here.'

'Done,' Adam replied.

Paris gladly let Adam lead her from Unger's office, down to the main floor where a crowd was steadily gathering, awaiting the start of the basketball game.

He stopped and spoke briefly to a man she assumed was Johnston, before he turned to her once more. Paris felt her heart kick against her rib cage at the serious expression she could see on his face.

'I have to go. The team needs me,' he said softly. 'Tonight's game is important to these kids, and when I tell them the coach and three of their players are out of the picture, it will be a blow to their confidence.'

'Can I do anything to help?' she asked, love and admiration welling up

261

inside her for this man who gave of himself so unselfishly.

Adam touched her cheek gently with his knuckles.

'Cheer for the team,' he said, 'and would it be too much to ask you to wait for me here, when the game's over?' His eyes held hers for a long breathless moment.

'I'll be here,' Paris said, and was instantly rewarded with a stunning smile that set her heart tripping over itself in excitement, before he turned and disappeared into the crowd.

For several seconds Paris didn't move, waiting for her heartbeat to return to normal and trying to come to grips with all that had happened since he'd found her.

She wondered for a moment if it had all been a bad dream. Then she recalled, with a shiver, the long cold night and the fear that she'd never be found.

Someone jostled her, effectively breaking into her reverie and Paris quickly made her way to the ticket counter. The smell of popcorn and hotdogs assaulted her, reminding her that she hadn't eaten all day, but when she realized her purse was still down in the locker room, she knew she'd rather starve than go back for it.

When she found a seat in the bleachers a little while later, the air of excitement building around her was almost tangible.

During the first quarter of the game, the Bears seemed listless and totally lacking in concentration, making foolish errors that cost them dearly.

When the fans in the gymnasium shouted their disapproval, her heart went out to Adam and the players, knowing full well the team's poor performance was a direct result of the news Adam had bestowed on them. By the end of the first half, the Richmond Rogues were leading by eighteen points.

But right from the moment the whistle blew for the start of the fourth quarter, Paris quickly noticed a change in the Bears' play, and the student who appeared to be picking up the pace of the game and taking charge of the play was Neil Pavan.

The fans immediately responded to his efforts, erupting in a frenzy of noise each time he scored. This, in turn, seemed to incite the team to try harder, and as the game speedily drew to its conclusion, the Bears had fought back to bring them within three points of the Rogues.

When Adam called a time-out with less than a minute to the final whistle, Paris couldn't hear herself think for the tremendous noise vibrating through the building.

The team stood in a huddle around Adam and when they ran back to their positions, Paris held her breath as the time clock began to run down.

Seconds later, the Bears scored, bringing them to within one point. The crowd let out a roar that shook the foundations. But with only seconds left in the game and the Rogues in possession of the ball, hope of a victory seemed to be lost.

Suddenly, Neil Pavan jumped up and intercepted a Rogue pass, and almost before anyone realized what was happening he'd turned and in one fluid motion threw the ball toward the hoop.

The ball slid through to score the winning basket just as the time clock ran out, and the fans erupted in an ear-shattering cheer that should have lifted the roof.

Pandemonium broke out around her and on the floor, and she cheered along with her neighbors as the team poured off the bench and grabbed Neil, lifting him high in the air. Through the crowd, she glimpsed Adam as he crossed to the Rogues' bench to shake hands with their coach.

It was some time before the noise in the gymnasium began to die down. No one seemed in a hurry to leave, and Paris made slow progress as she inched her way to where Adam had asked her to wait for him.

As she stood in the outer hallway waiting for Adam, a warmth and joy settled over her and her heart filled with anticipation.

But when the last few fans left the building, she began to wonder if Adam had forgotten about her.

12

'I'm sorry, Paris.' Adam's voice startled her, sending her heart skipping crazily inside her breast. 'It's pandemonium in the dressing room. I had a heck of a time getting out of there, then I stopped and put a quick call through to George and Lillian, to give them the rundown on all that's happened tonight.'

'Is George at home now?' Paris asked.

'Yes,' Adam replied. 'And I'm happy to say he's improving rapidly, especially now that he knows Unger has been arrested.'

'Did he know about Unger?'

'He had his suspicions. That's why he asked the police to investigate,' Adam said. 'But unfortunately, before George could fill me in on what was going on, he suffered a heart attack. That messed things up — in more ways than one,' he added ruefully.

'Did you tell him the Bears won?' she asked, as they began to walk toward the exit.

'Yes. Then he asked if I wanted my old coaching job back,' Adam said, a hint of laughter in his voice.

'The team must be on cloud nine, especially Neil. He did an amazing job.'

'Incredible. With the natural ability he has, he's going places. He asked me during the half-time break what happened to Unger and the others. After I explained, he said he'd thought for a while something was haywire with the coach . . . but he didn't know what to do, or who he should talk to.'

'And being his first year here, he was probably afraid no one would believe him,' Paris said, remembering the night he'd been waiting for her in the parking lot. Perhaps he'd planned to talk to her about it then.

'It's over now,' Adam said with obvious relief. 'And those kids came through in the crunch. I think you could say they're on cloud ninety-nine,' he added, as he held the door for her and they walked out into the cold, starry night.

'I don't think I've ever watched a more exciting game,' Paris went on.

'Exciting? Nerve-racking describes it better,' Adam said with fervor. 'Now I know why I gave up coaching. The pressure is incredible.'

Paris glanced at Adam, seeing the lines of fatigue on his face. 'You must be exhausted . . . ' she said, suddenly feeling awkward.

Adam came to a halt on the path and taking her hand in his, he turned her to face him, gazing intently into her eyes. 'I think it's time we settled the past, once and for all,' he said softly.

'Yes,' Paris said a little breathlessly, her pulse picking up speed in response to the look in his eyes and the touch of his hand.

The lights from the surrounding buildings cast shadows across his face, creating a mysterious look that only enhanced his attractiveness and sent a shiver of need racing through her.

He seemed to be waiting for her to speak, and so she drew a steadying breath and threw caution to the wind. 'I owe you an apology, Adam,' she said, and instantly she saw something flicker in the golden depths of his eyes. 'I was wrong to think you were to blame for what happened to Francesca. I realize now that I must have jumped to all the wrong conclusions . . . '

'Have you been talking to Lillian?' Adam cut in, his question surprising her.

'No . . . why?'

'Who have you been talking to . . . Francesca?' he asked, his tone suddenly urgent.

'I haven't been talking to anyone,' she told him.

'Then what made you change your mind?' he asked quietly, his gaze still intent on hers.

Paris hesitated, but only for a second. She'd come this far, and he deserved an explanation. Besides, what had she to lose? 'During the past few weeks, I've learned a lot about you, Adam. You're a kind, considerate, and generous man, a man who readily puts the needs of others before his own.

'I was a stranger here, yet it seemed that every time I needed help, you were there. And even when you knew that I believed you were responsible for Francesca's troubles, you still gave me your support unstintingly. And suddenly, I realized that I'd been wrong about you — you couldn't walk away from anyone in need of help, if your life depended on it.'

Adam was silent for a long time, and Paris felt as if her heart was being squeezed in a vise.

'Would you like to know the truth about Francesca?' Adam asked, finally breaking the silence.

Paris could only nod, knowing it was a ghost that needed to be laid to rest, but afraid to speak for fear he would change his mind.

'Francesca used to hang around the

basketball team. She came to all the practices and smiled and flirted with the players, and with me,' he began. 'I didn't pay too much attention at first, because she hung around with one of the players most of the time, but when she started to find excuses to come into my office, I began to wonder if she had a crush on me.' He stopped and ran a hand through his hair.

'One night after a game in the gym, I went back to my office to find her waiting for me. She'd been drinking . . . and to cut a very long story short, I told her to go home — that I wasn't interested. She got very angry, then she stormed out.

'About a month later, she came to my office a second time. She told me she was pregnant and that unless I agreed to marry her she'd go to the directors of the college and tell them I'd seduced her.

'I was stunned. But I told her I wouldn't be blackmailed, and that she should talk to the real father. That's when she broke down and I realized how emotionally distraught she must have been to come and accuse me.

'She told me Billy Ray, one of the players on the team, was the father, but when she'd told Billy about the baby, he'd said it was her problem and he'd have nothing to do with her.

'I offered to talk to Billy and she seemed relieved, but what I didn't know then was that rumors about Francesca and me had already started making the rounds.

'I talked to Billy, but he denied everything. I called Francesca and said I'd come by and talk to her. I wanted to see if I could persuade her to go somewhere for counseling. When I look back now, going to her house wasn't a good move on my part — it only fueled the rumors. But I couldn't tell her about Billy over the phone.' Adam stopped once more and gazed unseeingly into the night, a pained expression on his face.

Paris ached to touch him, to comfort

him as he'd tried to comfort Francesca, but she didn't move, waiting for him to finish.

'Your aunt let me in,' Adam said, 'but when I told Francesca about Billy she became hysterical. She started saying I had to marry her . . . that she'd take me to court . . . ' He shook his head at the memory. 'I came down pretty hard on her, but when she finally calmed down, I told her I'd bring someone she could talk to . . . and that I'd help her as much as I could.' He was silent for a moment and Paris picked up the story.

'I was hiding at the top of the stairs that day,' she said, 'you saw me. I was watching and listening, trying to figure out what was going on.' Fresh feelings of guilt washed over her at the memory. 'I only heard snippets, but at the time it was enough to make me believe you were walking out on her — that you were the one responsible for her unhappiness.'

'I came back a few days later,' Adam

went on. 'I brought a social worker with me . . . '

'I was back in Florida by then,' Paris explained. 'My parents had come to collect me. It was months before my mother received a letter saying Francesca had lost the baby and they were leaving for Europe.'

'And that's all you were told?' Adam asked disbelievingly.

'That's all,' Paris replied.

'No wonder you thought I was the villain,' he said, and once again Paris was amazed by his generosity and depth of understanding.

'Lillian said Francesca almost ruined your career . . . was that because of the rumors?' Paris asked.

'Yes, but to her credit Francesca went before the board of directors and told them she'd lied about my involvement.'

'If only I'd known . . . ' Paris said softly, regret in every syllable. 'I'm sorry . . . '

Adam put his finger under her chin and gently urged her to look at him.

'It's in the past, where it belongs,' he said, effectively closing the pages of a chapter which had played a significant part in both their lives. 'Right now, I'm far more interested in the present . . . and the future.'

Paris could scarcely breathe when she glimpsed the heat smoldering in his eyes.

'The future?' she said in a throaty whisper.

'There's a beautiful woman, an English teacher, I believe,' he said his tone light and teasing, now. 'I've become rather fond of her, and I was hoping you could put in a good word for me . . . maybe even find out what my chances are . . . '

Joy exploded through her, bringing tears to her eyes and making it almost impossible for her to speak. She swallowed the giant-sized lump in her throat. 'This is just a wild guess . . . ' she began, her voice wavering. 'And I could be jumping to conclusions . . . ' she went on. 'But, ah . . . the woman you mentioned. Is it me?'

''A wild guess,' she says. And who else would I be talking about?' Adam muttered, and Paris saw the merriment dancing in his eyes. He placed his hands on her shoulders, and she went very still. 'There is one small point I wish you would clarify,' he said, his tone serious now, 'before we take our first step into the future.' His eyes were riveted on hers, and she could feel the tension in him. 'I need to know . . . '

'I love you, Adam,' Paris said with such sincerity and depth of feeling that she took his breath away, along with the last of his doubts.

'And I love you,' Adam said, moments before his mouth came down on hers in a kiss that rocketed them to a world that was theirs alone.

'I think I like this sport much better than basketball,' Adam said some time later, when they returned to earth. 'In fact, there are a few finer points I'd like to demonstrate, if you're willing to learn,' he added, planting a brief kiss on her nose.

Laughter bubbled up inside her and she smiled up at Adam, the man she loved with all her heart. 'Are you suggesting I need a coach?' she asked teasingly.

'Of course,' came the reply. 'And I'm applying for the job on a permanent basis,' he told her. 'But I think as a team, we'll go far. We're just the right combination.'

'A winning combination,' Paris said, seconds before his lips claimed hers once more.

We do hope that you have enjoyed reading this large print book.

Did you know that all of our titles are available for purchase?

We publish a wide range of high quality large print books including:
Romances, Mysteries, Classics
General Fiction
Non Fiction and Westerns

Special interest titles available in large print are:
The Little Oxford Dictionary
Music Book, Song Book
Hymn Book, Service Book

Also available from us courtesy of Oxford University Press:
Young Readers' Dictionary
(large print edition)
Young Readers' Thesaurus
(large print edition)

For further information or a free brochure, please contact us at:
Ulverscroft Large Print Books Ltd.,
The Green, Bradgate Road, Anstey,
Leicester, LE7 7FU, England.
Tel: (00 44) **0116 236 4325**
Fax: (00 44) **0116 234 0205**

WILD FOR LOVE

Carol MacLean

Polly is an ecologist, passionate and uncompromising about wildlife rights. Against all her principles she falls in love with Jake, heir to a London media empire, whose development company is about to destroy a beautiful marsh. But can love ever blossom between two such different people? As Polly battles to save the marsh and learns to compromise for love, Jake finally finds the life he has always desired . . .